REDEEMED

WOLF GATHERINGS, BOOK FOUR

BECCA JAMESON

Copyright © 2014 by Becca Jameson

All characters and events in this book are fictitious. And resemblance to actual persons living or dead is strictly coincidental.

All rights reserved.

No part of this book may be reproduced in any form or by any electronic or mechanical means, including information storage and retrieval systems, without written permission from the author, except for the use of brief quotations in a book review.

❦ Created with Vellum

ACKNOWLEDGMENTS

To Lisa Dugan for all her hard work getting my books ready for print! You are the best cheerleader a girl could have!

CHAPTER 1

Blood.

So much blood.

As though she were floating in the room, separated from her body, Ashley watched the blood drip off her fingers and land on the tile floor. Each plop rang in her ears, amplified by the silence now reigning in her studio.

Moments ago the house had been filled with her screams, the loud pulsing of her own blood as it flowed through her ears, the grunts and groans of her attacker as he'd attempted to dominate her with his strength.

Now it was over. Silence. And blood.

She heaved for breath as her hands began to shake. She willed herself to release the knife, and it clamored to the floor, bouncing twice with a ping that made her flinch.

Oh God, I killed him.

The reality of her actions sank in as she stood rooted

to the spot, unable to move an inch. Her legs wouldn't respond to any of the messages her brain fired at them.

She stared in disbelief at the man on the ground at her feet. Damon Parkfield. She felt not one ounce of remorse for her actions. Should she?

Concern for the repercussions yes, but not sadness or sorrow. If she had to go to jail for the rest of her life for this killing, so be it.

Sirens wailed outside. She jerked her head up at the sound. The sirens got louder and multiplied.

She narrowed her gaze, knowing instinctively they were coming for her.

Damon entered her home less than half an hour ago. The cops were fast.

His downfall: she'd been anticipating him. She'd known he would come for her.

No longer the weak girl he'd held captive for four years, Ashley's mind had cleared. Her ability to think rationally had returned in bits and pieces over the past months. She'd visualized every imaginable scenario of this moment.

She'd known he would come eventually. Never for a second had she doubted his tenaciousness. Neither a restraining order nor the passage of time would keep Damon from seeking revenge.

"You're mine, bitch." His words still rang in her head. But Ashley's head was no longer floating in the clouds as she had been for the four years he'd tortured her. Nothing he could say would have altered the course of her actions.

What he didn't consider was her determination not

to be taken by him a second time outweighed his resolve to abduct her and hold her under his thumb once again.

The sound of police cars surrounding the house increased. Tires squealed and she closed her eyes, picturing the red and blue flashing lights spinning on the tops of several cruisers, skidding up to the curb, heedless of their haphazard parking jobs.

Doors slammed and she jerked again, her feet still rooted to the spot.

She opened her eyes and returned her gaze to the man on the floor, the bastard who'd stolen so much from her. All that would end now. No matter what happened next, she would never have to worry about Damon Parkfield again. And neither would any other woman...

CHAPTER 2

Six months earlier

A door slammed. Ashley slunk into the corner, covering her head with her arms. She couldn't get small enough, couldn't block out the sound of footsteps as they stomped to the basement, couldn't squeeze her eyes tight enough to keep out the light of day.

"You, bitch." Damon's voice barreled down the stairs and dispersed into every crack and crevasse in the damp space, seeping into the ancient beige couch she hovered behind as though the torn and unraveling upholstery soaked up each booming bellow and stored them to torment her later.

Ashley ducked her head farther, hoping to become invisible, or at least protect her skull from his wrath. Her bare foot slipped on the cracked concrete floor and she struggled to tuck it back under her thin white cotton nightgown.

"Where are you, Ash-ley?" He enunciated her name with the two distinct mocking syllables that grated on her nerves.

He stepped closer, his shuffling feet approaching from the base of the steps.

She knew exactly where he stood without looking. She could hear his breaths as they expelled in rapid succession.

"Ah, ain't that cute?" He ducked down beside her as soon as he came around the couch, the sound of his voice reaching her ears from way too close. "Did I scare you?" His words dripped with sarcasm and sugar.

When he set a gentle hand on her shoulder and stroked her bare skin, she withheld a flinch. His tone and his touch were a lie. Even though he petted her seemingly reverently as someone would caress a puppy, his hand was rigid, his fingers inflexible.

And then he struck—as she'd known he would. In the blink of an eye, she went from hovering in the corner to standing on her tiptoes with her back to the dank concrete wall of the unfinished basement.

Damon grabbed her wrists and yanked her upright by the arms until he held them high above her head, forcing her to suck in a breath and wait for the next blow.

There was always a next blow.

"Look at me, you whore." He spat the words across her forehead as she attempted to hide behind the locks of her lank unkempt hair that hung more like dreadlocks in front of her face than the gorgeous tresses she'd always been praised for in her youth.

Ashley lifted her gaze. To do otherwise would only further her detriment.

Whatever she'd done this time had royally pissed him off. It wasn't a difficult task.

"You called your fucking parents from the landline? What the hell were you thinking?"

Oh shit. How had he found that out? She swallowed, but her mouth was so dry she only managed to get her tongue stuck to the roof. "I'm sorry, Sir. I—"

"Do you realize what this means? Do you?" His voice rose as he screamed. "Now we have to move again. I don't want those damn pack members of yours meddling in our business. You're mine. My mate. And you'll damn well do as I say." He tucked one of her wrists under the other and gripped them both with one hand. And then he slapped her hard across the face with his free hand.

The instant sting burned deep in her jaw. It wasn't the first time he'd hit her face, but he didn't do so often, so it surprised her. Before she could inhale her next breath, he slapped her again. This time her lip cracked and blood trickled into her mouth, the metallic taste making her gag.

Jerking her wrists with one hand, Damon hauled her body around the worn couch and sat. Ashley whimpered. She hated making any sound when he acted like this, but she couldn't help it. Her head spun from the two blows, her brain muddled from slamming into her skull.

Damon yanked her across his lap, her belly landing so hard against his thighs the wind was knocked out of her. Her face slammed into the side of his shin and her feet flung out from under her to flail in the air, unable to keep purchase on the damp floor.

No. Oh God, no.

Damon still held her wrists together, forcing her arms toward the floor.

Blood dripped from her broken lip and mixed with the

tears of fear running down to her chin as she bucked her head.

It was no use. She had no strength to fight him. Damon was twice her size and whatever he was drugging her with zapped all the energy from her body.

This time he went for her buttock—his favorite. He whipped her nightgown up around her waist, exposing her naked ass to the air. Before one breath and the next, he jabbed the needle she'd grown accustomed to into the waning flesh of her butt and emptied the contents of the syringe into her battered body.

Ashley had no idea what he was drugging her with, but it worked. The fight deserted her body and she went limp against his legs. Drool ran from her mouth and she watched as pink drips landed on the concrete, a mixed of her blood, tears, and saliva.

Limp like a rag doll, she could do nothing as Damon stood and set her broken body on the couch. He didn't bother to pull her nightgown down over her exposed rump. And she didn't have the energy to do so herself.

She hadn't been given panties or a bra in months. The worn white cotton sleeveless nightie was her only clothing.

Her eyes grew heavier by the second as she watched him scamper around the room, gathering up items and stuffing them in a box. He muttered under his breath about how much trouble she was. "Fucking cunt. Why did I bother? The bitch can't do anything right. Can't even get pregnant and bear me some offspring. What's the matter with your goddamn female parts anyway, bitch?" He turned toward her.

She widened her heavy eyes. Held her breath. Thanked God she hadn't gotten pregnant any of the times he'd raped her. Even his wrath at her infertility was better than bringing a baby into this world to be tortured by this madman.

His voice rose as he spoke. "If you ever pull a stunt like that again, I'll slit the throats of every member of your family. Ya hear? That'll cut down on the chatting. You aren't to contact anyone without my permission. No one. If you can behave yourself and do as you're told, you might earn some privileges. But as long as I have to keep punishing you for your stupidity, you will find yourself locked in the cellar with not so much as a book to read for entertainment."

He returned to his task, ignoring her once again. The reprieve was welcome.

Ashley lowered her eyelids to small slits and watched him rummage around the room. She hated to completely let her guard down while he was in the house out of fear. But the drugs were making their way deeper into her bloodstream and soon she would lose the fight.

Damon dropped something, the crash dragging her back to the surface of lucidity. Whatever it was, he picked it up and flung it across the room in her direction. She couldn't move a muscle to get out of the way. It was large and heavy and it was about to hit her in the face...

Ashley screamed. She screamed so loud she shook herself out of a deep sleep and sat upright in bed. The thick layer of covers weighing her body down were too heavy and claustrophobic and she kicked at them to remove the pressure from her legs as she continued to scream. "No. Get off me!"

The door to her room slammed open and she jerked

her gaze to the entrance, fully expecting to see Damon standing there, a syringe in his hand.

Instead she found her mother running across the room, tugging on a robe. "Ashley," her voice was firm and loud. "You're okay. You're home. You're safe. No one is going to hurt you." She plopped onto the mattress beside her daughter and set a hand on Ashley's shoulder before Ashley could recover her wits and absorb her surroundings.

Eyes wide, she glanced around her childhood room, exactly as she'd left it four and a half years ago when she'd been kidnapped and dragged across the country by Damon Parkfield.

It was a dream from years ago. She was home. She'd been home for six months now.

She heaved for oxygen as her mind wrapped around her new reality. Yes, she was home. Indeed, she was not in that dank basement or any of the other places he'd kept her over the years. But she was far from safe... No, that bastard would never let her go. Until he was dead and buried, she would never be safe again...

Damon sat bolt upright in bed and glanced around the darkness at the hovel he'd called home for only three weeks this time. What had woken him?

A piercing ring yanked his gaze to the bedside table. His phone. *Fuck*.

Phone calls in the middle of the night were never

good news. They usually meant it was time to move again.

He grabbed the device and pushed the talk button before it could make that God-awful shrill again. "What?"

"Time to move. Get your shit together and be out of there before sunrise. I'll call back with directions when I have them. Get on the next bus to wherever and we'll go from there."

"Seriously?" He pushed the sheets away from him and stood, running a hand through his hair. "Again? I haven't fucking unpacked yet from the last move." *Why bother?*

A few moments of silence passed before the caller continued in his deep serious voice. "You want to get caught?"

Damon didn't reply.

"Listen, you know we're sorry you got such a bum deal here. And we're doing everything in our power to fix the situation, but you have to be more cooperative. Without us, you have nothing. Who the hell is bankrolling your ass? Do you hear me? You are one lucky bastard that we don't hang you out to dry and wipe our hands of you." His voice rose with each syllable. "Now, if you want to keep living as a free man, you'll get your ass out of bed and do as I say."

A click sounded and Damon flinched. He tossed the fucking cell on the bed and paced the room. The asshole was right. Whoever he was and the goddamn people he worked with who referred to themselves as the Romulus, when they said run, Damon said how fucking far this time? He had no choice. He couldn't prove anything. People were looking for him. He didn't know who they were, but if they found him it couldn't end well.

He had no idea who was behind this…thing. And he wouldn't be able to prove a word of his ridiculous story if he was hauled in for questioning. Who would believe him?

He was an idiot. He never should have agreed to this fucking farce in the first place. He'd been fine living alone. Why he'd ever succumbed to the temptation of taking on a woman he would never know. But when these fuckers came to him years ago, promising him a mate, descendants, hope to start his own pack—well, he'd caved and taken the bait.

Now he could kick himself every single day. He had no idea who had caused this clusterfuck, but he was stuck now.

If he gave up, there was no telling what fate awaited him. Whoever was following him so diligently from place to place was determined. They could be from The Head Council. Or maybe someone Ashley's family hired to find him after she'd escaped. Or, hell, as far as he knew, the very bastards who'd set up this disaster could be the ones driving him mad with their antics. Maybe no one was chasing him at all.

Whatever the case, he needed to move and move fast. He had no one to trust except the mysterious callers. To do otherwise could be detrimental.

He took a deep breath and began gathering his shit,

what little there was. He hadn't been kidding. Most was still in the duffle he carried from place to place.

All he could do was hope these people weren't jerking his chain and were true to their word. So far they'd done nothing but fuck with his life. They had better come through with a new mate and a permanent home and fast…

CHAPTER 3

"Ashley, how have you been feeling?" Dr. Parman's soft voice shook Ashley from her reverie.

She'd been staring out the window of the tenth floor office in a daze. She turned her gaze toward the sweet, middle-aged brunette woman who sat across from her in the plush burgundy armchair. "Okay, I guess."

"More nightmares?"

"Yes." She glanced at her lap and tucked her legs under her a little tighter. "But they're spreading out. Only about once a week now."

"It's normal, you know. It's called posttraumatic stress disorder. It's common for soldiers returning from war or anyone who undergoes a trauma such as yours."

"Yeah, yeah, I know. I've read all the research." Ashley fiddled with her fingers in her lap, popping her knuckles at every joint imaginable.

"I wish you'd reconsider joining a rape survivor support group. I think it would help you to share with others who have lived through similar circumstances."

Ashley shook her head. "No one has a story like mine. And besides I don't want to rehash this over and over. I want to move on." She attempted a grin.

Whatever the drug was Damon had given her for four years, it had left her discombobulated on many occasions. The bastard was such a coward he preferred to fuck Ashley while she couldn't fight back.

"It's true that I can't say I've met anyone who has undergone the level of abuse you have, but that doesn't mean there aren't people out there who could empathize with you."

Ashley said nothing.

Dr. Parman changed the subject. "Have you gotten out of the house?"

"No." And there was no fucking way she was going anywhere until Damon was found and arrested. Fear held her captive. A very real fear that couldn't be denied, not even by Dr. Parman. If Damon was lurking anywhere nearby waiting for her to leave the house alone, he was going to have to wait until hell froze over.

"You can't live your life in limbo, Ashley. Eventually you are going to have to face the fact he may never be found and go on with your life."

No, I don't. As far as Ashley was concerned, she'd been living in a sort of suspended animation for six months, ever since her brother and his mates had barged into her apartment and rescued her from the hell she'd been living for so many years she no longer really remembered her life before Damon.

Dazed and confused from the strange cocktail she'd received via syringe, she'd barely understood the implication of her rescue. An analysis of her blood had shown she'd received a strange blend of Rohypnol no one was familiar with. Even though the blood samples had been studied by doctors in the shifter world, none of them had ever seen a concoction quite like it before.

Whatever it was, it left her tired and disoriented for several days after an injection and then malleable for weeks. As she'd begun to comprehend the effects of the drug, she'd played along with the game, faking fealty to Damon to avoid the next injection and actually managing to postpone each dose until they'd grown farther and farther apart.

Dr. Parman continued when Ashley didn't respond. "Is your brother still asking you to come to his house for dinner?"

"Yes." He'd nagged her for months. But she wasn't ready to venture out at night. Most days she remained in the house with her mother while her father worked. She managed to come to the appointments with her psychologist, but that was about it. No trips to the store and no nights out on the town.

The less exposure she had, the less often she hyperventilated. The only reason she'd agreed to visit the psychologist was because her family had found one who was a member of the wolf-shifter community.

"Perhaps if he picked you up and returned you home, you'd be able to take that step?"

"I'll think about it." She bit her lip and stared at Dr. Parman. She knew she was a tough case, not easily cracked. The evidence of her difficulty sometimes presented itself in the corners of her doctor's eyes. But the woman never gave up.

"Have you shifted since you've been home?"

"No." Ashley shook her head. She hadn't shifted in several years in fact. She was beginning to worry if she even could.

Dr. Parman leaned forward and set her elbows on her knees. "I'm sure your brother and his mates would be willing to take you someplace secure and assist you with the transition."

"I'm not ready," she deadpanned. *I may never be ready.*

"Let's talk about the dreams. Has anything changed?"

Ashley took a deep breath and began to describe last night's episode of "Who wants to make Ashley crazy while she sleeps?"

Josh reached out in the dark of night and wrapped his arms around his mate. Samantha snuggled in closer, her warm breath wafting across his chest as she buried her face against him. Nathan slept soundly on the other side of her, oblivious to the turmoil disrupting Josh's sleep. In fact, Josh smiled as a soft snore filled the silence from Nathan's side of the bed. At least one of them could rest easy.

Josh hadn't rested well in years, not since his sister had disappeared from The Gathering and called home the next day from the road claiming she'd run off with her mate. Josh hadn't attended that Gathering, or any other for many years. Not since he'd been a child. But his family had been there. Whatever Ashley had said to his parents that fateful Sunday morning from the road had been convincing.

It wasn't altogether unusual for wolves to mate and run off together. They didn't often leave without saying goodbye, but wolves in the midst of a claiming could be incredibly selfish and single minded. It wasn't impossible to conceive.

Josh grinned. He'd been in that exact scenario six months ago when he'd met Samantha and then Nathan the weekend he'd finally located Ashley and rescued her from hell with the help of his PI, and now good friend, Evan.

Thank God for Evan. The man had worked tirelessly night and day to find Ashley and he'd come through after months of searching. Josh knew without a doubt he'd been undercharged for the job, but Evan had insisted finding Ashley and helping in her escape had been so gratifying they were even.

Josh and Evan had grown close over the course of months of working together. Unfortunately Evan had been knee deep in work ever since the rescue and barely had time for more than a chat on the phone. But Josh was bound and determined to lure the man over with the promise of good food as soon as possible. If he was lucky, perhaps he could get Ashley out of the house at the same time and introduce her to the man who'd essentially saved her life.

"You're thinking so hard, I can't sleep." Samantha's sweet voice was deep and hoarse from slumber.

He kissed the top of her head and then tipped her

chin up to look into her eyes. It was darker than usual in the room, the moon absent, but his wolf senses didn't keep him from seeing Samantha's clear blue eyes and the smile that spread across her face. "Sorry," he whispered, not wanting to wake Nathan. "Didn't mean to wake you."

"You're worried about Ashley."

She didn't have to ask. She knew him well. And he loved her for it. He nodded.

"I'll go over soon and spend some time with her. How about this weekend? I don't have to work Saturday. I'll go see what kind of progress she's making. But, Josh, don't worry so much. She's coming along. Every time I see her, she's better. It's going to take time. I'm impressed with her clarity after only six months. She has a deep understanding of what happened to her and a fine head on her shoulders. She's even taking some online classes to start working on her art degree."

"Good. Thanks, baby. I appreciate everything you do for my sister. It's above and beyond."

She slapped at him playfully, her voice lower when she spoke. "She's my sister too now, and I love her as much as I love all your family members. Helping her is not a hardship. She's a wonderful woman and she will pull through this and succeed in life. Mark my words."

Nathan rolled over at that moment and wrapped his arm around both of them. His fingers dangled across Josh's chest, and their presence no longer made Josh freak out to be touched by a man. They were mates. They didn't fuck each other, but they did touch while they loved Samantha and it no longer held the weird factor as it had in the beginning.

None of the three of them expected a claiming that involved an extra shifter, but over time they'd gradually accepted the odd relationship, moved into Josh's house, and forged a bond stronger than any mated pair ever had.

"Are you guys solving world hunger in the middle of the night again?" Nathan's voice was rough and full of teasing.

"Yep," Samantha said, "and we've decided to send you on a tour of the world passing out MREs."

"Oh, good. Can I leave soon? This case I'm working on is killing me."

Josh sighed. That was the truth. Like Samantha, Nathan was an attorney. He'd been working with some high-powered secret client for weeks and hadn't been home much. Neither Josh nor Samantha were upset about his absence. It wasn't avoidable. But they missed his part in their family dynamic when he wasn't around. "Sorry we woke you. Samantha claims she can't sleep when I'm thinking too hard." He chuckled.

"It's true. Don't deny it. I can sense your stress even when I'm dead asleep. Especially when you're worrying about Ashley." Samantha kissed his chest and laid her head against him once more. She grabbed the hand Nathan had draped over them and gripped his fingers tight.

Josh took a deep breath. "Is there anything else we can do—legally?"

Nathan lifted his face to stare at Josh over

Samantha's head. "No, but we could hire Evan to hunt down Damon. I know Ashley's progress is stymied by the fact that her fucked-up ex is still out there roaming the streets. The police don't have the manpower to look for a man all over the country who isn't currently committing a crime. Why don't you ask Evan if he's available to help find Damon?"

"Not a bad idea. Though it's hard to nail Evan down these days. I'll see if I can get him tomorrow by cell."

Samantha patted Josh's chest. "Good plan. You call Evan tomorrow. Let's try to get some sleep. It's almost three a.m. and we all have to work early."

Josh closed his eyes. The idea was promising. It was indisputable that Evan was good at his job. But could he track down Damon and would it help if he did? The last thing he wanted was for Evan to be in danger at the hands of this lunatic.

Deep even breaths. Think pleasant thoughts about running in wolf form in the woods, Nathan and Samantha at your side. That's perfect...

Finally, he let his eyes droop until he drifted off, his last thought one of the three of them rushing through the trees. He wasn't sure if they were chasing something or being chased, but he fell asleep anyway, praying for a miracle.

CHAPTER 4

Evan stared out the window, leaning his forehead against the cold pane of glass and trying desperately to concentrate on work. He watched as hundreds of people scurried around seven stories below like ants in a maze. Everywhere he looked he found a frenzy of folks hurrying to somewhere.

Meanwhile, his life was stuck on hold. He felt like a freeze frame, like someone took a snapshot of his world six months ago and froze it in time. His eyes could move and the earth kept revolving and tugging him along with it, but his heart and soul were stuck in a holding pattern.

The cool glass of the window helped center him. He could watch humanity below as though through a lens without getting too close to anyone.

Damn Fate and Her strange sense of humor. Her choice in this instance was not remotely humorous.

Evan's cell rang, making him flinch. He turned

toward his desk and grabbed the phone to see who the caller was. If a person could smile and frown at the same time, Evan had it mastered.

Joshua Rice.

"Hey," Evan said as he connected.

"Hey, yourself. How are you?"

"Good. Been busy at work." Evan chuckled, though he doubted it sounded sincere, especially since it wasn't. "Making this transition has increased my hours instead of decreasing them. Why did I think it would make my life easier?"

Months ago Evan made the decision to turn his one-man private investigator gig into a business with staff. The end goal had been to keep himself in town and hire others to do the traveling. Plus it freed him up to work on the one case that drove him completely crazy. It had worked and business was booming, but Evan put in long hours to ensure everything ran smoothly. He wasn't the best delegator.

"Yeah, that's generally how it works, unfortunately. Listen, I haven't seen you in ages. I'm planning a little dinner party. I hope you'll come."

"Of course. When is it?" It wasn't like he could use the excuse he was out of town. Josh knew he didn't travel anymore. And he had to stop putting the man off. The reality was, he really liked Josh. Hell, he even liked Nathan, the man Josh shared his mate with.

"Saturday night. Seven."

"Sounds good. Let me double check my schedule and I'll get back to you." Evan stared at the blank calendar on his desk, the one that had nothing scheduled for him besides work for the next fifty years.

"Great. There'll be about a dozen of us. I'm hoping to get Ashley here too." Josh's words were casual. Bits of information to make small talk.

Evan's reactions were not casual. The name Ashley alone made him stiffen. His cock jerked to attention and his pulse leaped to a new height. "Sounds good. I'll call you back later today." *After I find my brain cells and pull them together to ponder this proposition.*

"All right. Talk to you soon."

"'Bye, man." Evan set the phone on his desk soundlessly and stared into space, seeing nothing. His chest pounded. Should he go?

Ashley. The woman who had stolen his heart and kept him in this perpetual state of unrest ever since.

He'd only seen her one time and that had been six months ago. One hundred eighty-four days, but who was counting? The day he'd helped rescue her from Damon Parkfield's clutches. Thank God he hadn't been alone. Josh, Nathan, and their mate Samantha had been at the apartment where they'd finally nailed down Ashley's location.

The moment the woman opened the door, Evan had known she was his. It had taken all the strength he could muster to avoid grabbing her and running. Instead, he'd stepped back and let her brother and his mates convince her to leave with them.

Fists in two tight balls, he'd managed to keep from punching a hole in the door to her apartment. Flimsy as it was, he probably would have found his arm stuck all the way through.

He knew she hadn't realized she was his. She'd been broken and abused, drugged and confused. Evan held his tongue and kept this secret to himself.

Ashley needed time. She needed to heal and separate herself from the bastard who terrorized her for four long years. She couldn't have faced the fact she belonged to Evan on top of everything else. So, Evan stepped aside. He'd turned down every invitation from Josh that might have included Ashley and kept this deep painful secret buried inside.

Meanwhile, unbeknownst to Josh and his family, Evan had been searching for Damon. Eventually the man would pay and pay dearly. He deserved to rot in the fifth circle of Hell for all eternity, but that would be too easy. Evan wanted him alive to spend his days in jail pondering what he'd done to the sweet young girl he'd kidnapped and held hostage for all those years.

Damon was sneaky though. He moved a lot. He'd slipped through Evan's fingers several times. Evan wished like hell he'd known how bad it had been for Ashley the day they'd found her. If so, he never would have left the apartment. He'd have stayed and taken Damon down that very day.

The hesitation had ruined his chances. By the time Evan returned, Damon was long gone, having left no trail.

Evan pushed away from the desk and stood once more. He suffered from anxiety these days. He couldn't sit long. Knowing his mate was out there, knowing who she was and where she lived, kept him in a state of unrest that wouldn't abate.

Perhaps it was time to face her. Even if she wasn't ready to deal with the knowledge yet, at least Evan wouldn't be alone. He felt confident that if he walked into a room she occupied, she'd know about her fate within moments.

Was that playing fair? It had been half a year. Evan couldn't begin to guess if that was enough time, but by all accounts from Josh, his sister was doing well. She was strong and determined. She was taking classes online and seeing old friends. She just didn't leave the house often.

He could understand that. Who would want to wander around in the world knowing some jackass might attack them at any moment?

Ashley's hands shook as she entered her brother's home on Friday night. She agreed to attend Josh's dinner party, but it didn't change the fact that nerves ate her from the inside out. She didn't want to become a recluse, but it took great courage to go out, especially at night, while Damon was still on the loose.

Granted, he might never be found, and there was always the chance he wasn't interested in Ashley anymore. After all, she hadn't been the perfect mate to him. She'd been less than docile and hadn't managed to bear him any offspring. If she was lucky, he'd moved on and given up on her.

But, if she wasn't lucky…

She wiped her palms on her skirt as she handed Samantha her coat. The house smelled of Italian food. Simmering meat sauce filled her senses and made her stomach growl.

She smiled at her newest friend, Samantha, as the woman hugged her. Bless the woman for all she'd done to befriend Ashley in the last six months.

"I'm so glad you came," Samantha said. She set a hand on top of one of Ashley's and squeezed. "Relax and enjoy. No one is going to get into this house without our knowledge." She glanced behind Ashley toward the front door. "Did your parents drop you off?"

"Yes." Fundamentally, Ashley knew she was safe here. But anxiety had a way of overruling one's common sense. Dr. Parman had been more than willing to prescribe something for the anxiety, but after taking such strange mind-altering drugs for four years, Ashley couldn't bear to put something foreign into her system, even if her sanity was at stake.

No one quite knew what Damon had given her. It seemed to have completely left her body given time and there didn't appear to have been any long-term repercussions, but the substance remained a mystery. A vial of her blood was being studied at a lab run by shifters in Boston, but so far any inquiry about the drug had turned up nothing. No other pack around the United States had heard of anything like it.

Ashley smiled at Samantha. She appreciated the woman more than words could express, but she couldn't speak over the lump in her throat.

"Come on. Let me introduce you to everyone. They're all milling around in the kitchen, hoping to grab a bite before it's even fully cooked." Samantha took Ashley's hand and tugged, luring her into the noisy gathering of shifters.

At the door, Samantha cleared her throat to get everyone's attention. "Everyone, this is Ashley, Josh's sister."

The bright kitchen was filled with laughter and light. The appliances shown with their steel surfaces and the granite counter reflected the lighting to make the room inviting and warm.

Samantha pointed toward the first person on the right as she began her introductions. "Ashley, that's my brother Gabriel and his mate, Kathleen. Next to Kathleen is her sister, McKenzie, and her mate, Drake. The four of them are here on vacation for the week. They've never been to St. Louis and we haven't all been together since everyone mated. So, it's wild and crazy. Don't let their volume scare you." Samantha smiled warmly again and squeezed Ashley's arm.

"Nice to meet you all." Ashley looked around the room at the perfectly normal shifters. She envied them their carefree lives, but she needed to get past the sensation that she'd missed out on four years and make the most of the rest of her life.

The men bustled from the room when Josh bellowed something from the living room about football. Samantha excused herself for a moment, and Ashley was left with the two new women, Kathleen and McKenzie.

"Please, call me Kenzie." The woman on the left lifted her hand to greet Ashley.

Ashley smiled as she shook her hand and then Kathleen's. "Where do you live? Did you travel far?"

Kathleen spoke next. "Gabriel and I live in Houston. He's a doctor there." She thumbed toward Kenzie. "Kenzie and Drake live on a ranch in northwest Texas. We haven't seen each other since we both mated at The Gathering seven months ago."

"That's nice—that you all could convene for a vacation together." Even hearing the words "The Gathering" made her flinch. Four and a half years ago at that very festivity she'd been kidnapped by Damon. Although she had repressed many days between then and now, some purposefully, some from a drug-induced haze, she remembered that day like it was yesterday. The details were never far from her mind.

"Are you okay?" Kathleen set a hand on Ashley's bicep, drawing her back to the present.

"Yes." She shook her memories away.

Kenzie lifted a bottle of wine. "Can I pour you a drink?"

Ashley shook her head. "No, thanks." She never touched alcohol. Anything that altered her mind or dampened her senses in any way made her run the other direction.

"There's soda and bottled water in the fridge if you want anything." Kathleen nodded toward the refrigerator.

The doorbell rang, making Ashley jump inside her

skin. She closed her eyes for a moment to give herself a pep talk.

It's another guest. Get ahold of yourself. Josh had said there would be nine people total so that left one more to arrive after Ashley.

She turned toward the living room, following Kenzie and Kathleen.

She didn't remember Evan, but she knew him to be the last person who would arrive. He was the private investigator who located her months ago, apparently after searching in many states over a long period of time. She owed him a thank you for all he'd done. At the time, she'd been so concerned about pissing off Damon, she'd paid no attention to the man who'd remained outside the apartment while Samantha, Josh, and Nathan helped her gather her meager belongings and scurry from the apartment before Damon could return.

A deep jovial voice came from the entry as Ashley rounded the corner. It calmed her for some reason she couldn't explain. Perhaps the idea a PI was attending the party would help her nerves. Surely he would be useful in an emergency.

The front door shut with a loud snick and Kathleen and Kenzie parted, giving Ashley her first glimpse at her savior.

The instant she laid eyes on him, she froze. Built like a linebacker with brown wavy hair, he filled the room. But that wasn't what sucked the air from her lungs. As he turned toward her, her suspicions were confirmed. Deep brown eyes penetrated her from across the room.

They wrinkled at the corners as he smiled in her direction.

All the shit she'd been through for the last several years, all the lies she'd been fed from Damon about being his mate, all the stories she'd heard from friends and family about what it felt like to meet one's mate—it all made sense in a heartbeat.

Evan Harmon was her mate.

CHAPTER 5

Evan stood very still as he let his mate soak in the information he knew was bombarding her. He hated that he'd arrived already one up on her. It wasn't fair. But it also wasn't avoidable. He'd made the decision to let the cat out of the bag, and there was no going back.

She was gorgeous. Her blonde hair hung in rivulets below her shoulders. It shown in the light and bounced when she stepped. He breathed a sigh of relief that it was fuller and healthier than the lank locks he'd seen on her the only other time he'd stared in her direction.

She'd been too skinny and sickly that day. Tonight she was better nourished from months of eating well and living without the drugs. Her green eyes blinked at him, pools of water he could see through—no longer dark and sunken.

Her cheeks pinkened as he watched, the glow making him smile.

"Evan?" Josh took his arm.

"Yeah. I'm sorry." The secret was out. There was no

way anyone in the room wouldn't catch the subtle nuances that declared two people to be mates.

"For what?" Josh stepped to the side into Evan's line of sight. Thankfully, he didn't block Ashley, whose eyes still gazed into Evan's. She hadn't flinched.

Silence. Everyone hushed.

"Oh." Josh gasped. "You knew."

"I did." He paid no attention to anyone else in the room. They were almost all strangers to him, and he didn't care. The only person who mattered, who would ever matter again in this lifetime, was Ashley. He cared only for her feelings and reactions.

"Why didn't you say anything? Oh God, it's been months."

"One hundred eighty-nine days," Evan muttered. "It wasn't a good time." He smiled and glanced at Josh. That was an understatement.

"Ashley?" Josh took about three steps to get to his sister's side. "Are you okay?"

She didn't move. She wouldn't be completely okay for a very long time, but Evan intended to ensure she eventually was whole and healthy and happy.

"Ash?" Josh continued, "Did you know too?"

She shook her head.

Samantha approached and tugged on Josh's arm. "Let's give them some time."

"But—" Josh was flustered. His mouth hung open.

"Josh," his mate soothed, "we must. Let's go in the kitchen and let them talk." She turned toward the others and motioned them all out of the room.

It was eerily quiet for several moments and Evan

pictured all seven people holding their breath in shock in the kitchen.

"I'm sorry," he repeated. "There was no easy way to handle this." He stepped toward Ashley, but not close enough to make her uncomfortable.

He'd worried about this meeting for so long he'd lost sleep most nights. His greatest fear was how he would handle her in such a delicate state. But now that he stood before her, all his doubt fluttered away. She was his mate. That was all that mattered. He'd do anything for her, including take things at whatever pace she needed. It wouldn't be the difficult task he'd envisioned. Nothing having to do with Ashley would ever be a challenge.

"Why? How?" she gasped.

"It wasn't easy." He smiled at her. "You needed time to heal."

"I'm not healed. I don't know if I ever will be." She shook her head as though she could deny their attraction with those words and actions.

"It's okay, Ashley. I understand. We'll work through it together. I'll be by your side the entire way."

He watched as her chest rose and fell under the weight of new problems she hadn't foreseen. Her breasts were high and full with the weight gain that made her look physically mended.

"You're beautiful," he said.

She blushed and ducked her gaze for the first time.

"Sit with me?" He motioned to the couch.

She shuffled that direction and took a seat on one far end, hugging the arm rest.

Evan kept his face straight, but grinned inwardly at her attempt to keep a distance. He wouldn't pressure her to do anything. In fact, he'd make no move until she was ready every step of the way.

"How are you feeling? Josh speaks of you pretty often, but tell me in your words." He sat in the center of the sofa, not close enough to force contact, but near enough to breathe her in.

"Okay, I guess. It's hard. Every day is a challenge. I'm nowhere near ready for—"

"Ashley, don't stress. I'm not going to push you. It may have been selfish of me to come here tonight, but I couldn't stand knowing this secret and carrying it alone for another day. I don't want you to read too much into my presence here tonight. I swear to you I will take things at whatever pace you need."

She lifted her gaze, peered into his eyes. "And what if that pace is to stop right here and never let it go any further?"

He'd anticipated such an answer. Hell, every possibility had gone through his mind over the months. She did have the right to reject him outright. It would be hard, but if it was what she wanted, he would grant her that concession. "If that's what you decide, then that's how it shall be. But I'd like you to at least give me a chance. Spend some time with me. Let me take some of the burden you've been carrying and get to know me."

"Sounds risky. You cloud my mind."

He grinned. "That's a good sign. At least we're even on that front." He leaned forward, careful to avoid touching her, and placed his elbows on his knees. "Get to know me. That's all I ask. It would hurt too much if we didn't at least try. I'd hate to live without knowing how it could have been."

"That's fair." Her hands shook as she set them on her lap and rubbed her palms on her skirt.

Evan glanced down at her legs. Dainty was the best way to describe her. She couldn't be more than about five four. At six feet he towered over her, even sitting. Any woman would be intimidated by him. "Would you like me to leave so you can enjoy your evening?"

"No." She shook her head. "Stay." Her words were emphatic. That was a good sign. Things were looking up already.

∼

Ashley's head spun as though she'd fallen and the concussion was making her dizzy. So many thoughts went past her consciousness she couldn't keep up with them.

This man was her mate. There was no doubt. The chemical attraction was so transparent she couldn't understand how she'd believed for a moment Damon had been her mate. He'd insisted. She'd always suspected there was a lot more to the bond between mates than Damon presented, but now the proof was obvious.

She'd never felt one ounce of attraction for Damon. This new man, Evan, called to her on an undeniable level. Her entire body lit up when he entered the house.

A deep yearning for something she never expected to have melted her insides and left her wobbly.

But she was ruined. Broken. Unfixable. No one should have to walk this path with her.

She'd agreed to give him a chance simply because she'd been too weak to turn him down. He'd stared at her with such deep brown eyes. She'd been a sucker for his finely chiseled jaw, the dark brown hair that fell across his forehead in a way that made her want to run her fingers through it.

Ashley closed her eyes and took a deep breath. She needed to get a grip. The impossible was right before her. A true mate.

She would have to let him down easy. No way in the world would she drag someone else into her hell on earth and force him to walk the path that lay before her.

She'd become a recluse, too chicken to leave the house. The fact that she'd come here tonight was a miracle in and of itself. When she'd have the courage to venture out again, she didn't know. She wouldn't be able to stop shaking until she was safely back in her room at her parents' house where the place was locked up like a fortress and surveillance cameras gave her a false sense of security.

She knew her fears were absurd, but they were hers and they were real and she owned them.

She stared at Evan's profile as they sat down to dinner. God, what she would give to have a man hold her during the night. Would she be able to sleep soundly for more than two hours if someone else held the reins and kept her safe from the boogeyman?

Everyone around her chatted as she remained silent. The meal was fantastic. She wished her throat would open up and allow her to eat more than the few bites she swallowed.

There was an elephant in the room and no one acknowledged it, bless them. She couldn't fathom the idea of discussing her new status with the group.

When the meal was over, the men headed for the living room and left the women sitting around the table.

Kenzie scooted over several chairs to sit across from Ashley. "I'm so sorry. I know my timing stinks tonight, but I need to talk to you about something." The woman fidgeted. She tapped her fingers on the table and paused before she continued. "Samantha told me a little about what happened to you. She said you were taken from The Gathering four years ago. Is that right?"

"Yes." Ashley was used to questions. She'd answered dozens but not often by someone she'd just met.

"I'm sorry to be so blunt. I know you must be going through some really tough times, but I think I might know something that could help."

Ashley furrowed her brow. How could Kenzie know anything new?

Kenzie visibly swallowed and leaned forward. Katherine and Samantha sat at the seats flanking her. They didn't seem shocked when Ashley glanced at the other women. They all knew what Kenzie was about to say.

"Did that man drag you to a dark room and rape you before he took you from The Gathering?" Her words were barely more than a whisper. It pained her to ask the question. She cringed as she waited for Ashley to respond.

Ashley opened her mouth, stunned by the question. How could anyone know that? She'd never told a soul about that night. It hurt too much and it wasn't relevant. So many things had happened over the years to make that event pale in comparison.

Kenzie's eyes watered and tears dripped from the corners to run down her face. She made no move to wipe them away.

Ashley swallowed finally and nodded. "He did." Her voice was hoarse as though she'd been crying for hours. "How did you know?" Her murmured words would barely be heard. She herself detected no sound coming from her mouth over the storm raging in her ears.

Kenzie glanced down at her hands and wrung them on the table top before she looked back up. "I was there... In the room."

Ashley's eyes shot wide open. Was that possible? The idea had never occurred to her.

Kenzie continued. "I was hiding from the world because I didn't want a mate. I was sitting by the far window in a tall armchair, curled up against the world. When the door burst open and that bastard dragged you inside, I was stunned. He didn't notice me and you were on the floor out of sight. I froze."

She paused. Ashley didn't know what to say.

"I've regretted my actions that night all these years and here you are, the very woman who was terrorized and taken against her will. I'm so sorry." She leaned forward but quickly ducked back and lowered her gaze as though she had no right. "If only—"

Ashley found her voice. "You couldn't have known."

"I was right there. It scared the hell out of me. I was only nineteen at the time. I was a coward."

"You were hardly more than a child. So was I. It wasn't your fault. I don't imagine I would have done anything differently if I'd been you."

"I never wanted to mate after witnessing that. It was absurd, but I worried there were other claimings that went that way. He was so mean. He—you don't need me to rehash what he did. Sorry."

Ashley tugged a smile from deep inside her. Somehow, even though she was forced to relive a moment she'd hoped never to conjure again, she was comforted by the fact this stranger had been there with her. It gave the act validity. No one, as far as she knew, had ever seen how Damon had treated her at any point. He'd been careful through the years to keep their unique relationship a secret from the world.

"Anyway, I only brought this up because I wanted you to know that if you ever need me… Like to testify or something, if they catch him, I'll be there for you. I won't let you down a second time."

Ashley set a hand on top of Kenzie's shaking grasp. They'd formed a bond of sorts. It was a small step, but for Ashley it was important. She had an ally. This woman knew some small part of what her life had been like. She was not alone.

Ashley smiled at Kenzie. "But you did find a mate. And you're pregnant." She glanced at Kenzie's lap, not completely sure how she knew that last part. It wasn't physically obvious yet. She knew wolves had sharp senses, but she'd never actually deduced something like a pregnancy before.

Kenzie grinned back. "I did. And I am." She set a hand over her stomach. The bulge was barely visible. "Three months. The baby is due in the summer."

"I'm so happy for you." Ashley held Kenzie's gaze. Now that they'd changed the subject to Kenzie's mate and baby, the woman's eyes nearly danced. Ashley would give anything in the world to feel as happy as Kenzie clearly felt.

CHAPTER 6

Evan watched his mate out of the corner of his eye. She sat in an intimate huddle with the other three ladies for a long time, though he couldn't hear anything they said.

From the living room, he could keep an eye on her and still pretend to be engrossed in the conversation with the four men.

Finally, Ashley stood and hugged all the women. He assumed she was planning to leave. No way was she leaving without him. Even if he had to woo her for months, she was his and their connection couldn't be denied.

Josh slapped him on the back and brought his attention to his friend. His eyes sparkled. "Will you take her home? I intended to, but it seems things have changed. If she agrees, that is."

"Of course." Evan waited while Josh headed to a bedroom to grab their coats.

Ashley approached him, her gaze nailing him to his spot. "I guess my brother asked you to give me a ride."

"He did. I would have insisted anyway." *Just so we're clear.*

He hadn't touched her and he knew he couldn't until she was ready. But he needed her to know they would be moving forward at her pace, not his. Hopefully that would erase the fear in her eyes.

Josh arrived with their coats. It was cold outside, a typical January winter day in St. Louis. She wore a skirt and he wished he'd heated the car before they went out. But she was already slipping her arms into the sleeves of her jacket.

"Take care of my sister, please." Josh gave Evan a glare. They were friends but Josh knew all too well what it was like when a man met his mate, and he was rightfully worried about his sister.

What he didn't know was Evan would never harm a hair on her head. He'd worship her for the rest of his life or walk away if she demanded it of him.

Without a word, Evan opened the front door and stepped outside. The ground was slippery. He turned toward Ashley and grabbed her arm before she could fall on the slick steps and the front walk. It was a gesture he would extend to any woman.

She flinched, but soon relaxed her muscles and allowed him to lead the way to his car. "Thanks. I'm useless in heels."

"I don't know why you women wear those things. Especially in this weather." He stared at her feet, wishing he could peel those shoes off and massage the muscles that would be tightened from the trapped confines.

Instead he jerked his gaze back toward the street and pressed the button to unlock his car. He drove a silver Infiniti G37, his baby. It would warm up fast and the seats were heated.

As quickly as he could, he opened the passenger door and waited while Ashley lowered herself into the seat. He shut the door and rounded the car at a jog. Damn, it was cold.

In moments he had the heater running and the seats warming. He rubbed his hands together and blew into the cup he'd formed with his palms.

Her teeth chattered and he doubted it was entirely from the temperature. He turned toward her. "I'd never pressure you, just so you know. Whatever happens between us is completely up to you, and we move at your pace. I'm not an ass. If I were, your brother never would have let me take you home." He lifted on eyebrow and grinned as he used his best logic on her.

"Okay." She leaned more comfortably into the seat, but didn't fully relax.

There wasn't a thing he could do but spend time with her. The only way for her to get to know him and trust him was to prove himself over and over until she believed.

The circumstances of this mating were less than ideal, but Fate didn't ask his opinion when She put Ashley in his path. She had Her reasons.

He pulled away from the curb and headed toward the highway.

"You haven't asked me for directions."

"I know where you live." He smiled at her.

"Of course."

"Not that I was stalking you, but I do know where you live."

She looked out the window, chewing on her lower lip. He could see her profile whenever he glanced her direction. She was hesitant to trust. Rightfully so.

It took about twenty minutes to arrive at her parents' home in West County. When he pulled up, he turned off the car and dashed around the hood to help her out.

"I'm a pretty good walker, you know."

"In those heels? I doubt it. I'd be remiss if I let you fall on your ass."

At the door, she pulled a set of keys from her purse, but before she could stick the key in the lock, the door swung open.

Ashley's father stood just inside, his smile fading as his gaze roamed over Evan. He did manage to step aside and permit them both entrance.

"Daddy, this is Evan. Evan, my father, Paul Rice."

Evan stuck his hand out to shake her father's as Ashley shut the door behind them. He wanted to fall into a hole the way the man was scrutinizing him. But it couldn't be helped. He'd known what he was up against before he'd agreed to this dinner party. The road ahead was a rough one, wrought with distrust on many levels. He had no choice but to be up to the task. After all, the prize was Ashley and to do anything else was unacceptable.

"Evan gave me a ride home. He's Josh's friend, the one who—"

"I know who he is. Come in. Sit. I'll get coffee." Paul pointed at the sofa as he passed through the room. *He knows.*

Evan had met with Paul and Laura Rice over a year ago when he'd taken over the investigation to find Ashley.

"I'm going to go, um…" Ashley pointed over her shoulder.

"Yes, you look exhausted. Go to bed. We'll talk tomorrow." Evan relaxed his shoulders as Ashley backed out of the room. Her sexy legs had goose bumps from the cold. Her cheeks were pink, though it was hard to know if that was from wind or nerves.

When she was out of sight, Evan sat. Slumped was more like it. He'd been tense for so many hours, he couldn't hold himself upright another moment.

Paul returned a few minutes later with his wife behind him. "Laura, you remember Evan." He set two steaming mugs on the coffee table.

Evan jumped to his feet. "Ma'am."

"You're the private investigator?"

"Yes, ma'am."

"How did you…? I mean—"

They were skirting what all three of them were actually thinking. It would have been comical, if this meeting of the parents weren't one of the most important meetings of Evan's life. "I was with Josh and his mates when we found Ashley, but I never went inside. She was…distraught. She probably never noticed I was there. The moment I realized who she was to me,

I backed off. I knew she wouldn't be prepared to deal with that bombshell, so I let her go."

"That took a lot of courage," Paul said.

"You have no idea." Evan smiled and resumed his spot on the couch as Ashley's parents also sat.

"So, what do you have in mind now?" Laura asked. She wrung her hands together the same way he'd seen her daughter do several times this evening.

"Nothing that Ashley doesn't expressly request. Don't worry about that. I have only her best interests in mind."

"What if she can't handle this...any of it?" Paul asked.

"Then I'll have no choice but to walk away. I'd never do anything to upset her or her progress toward healing."

Paul shook his head slowly. "That won't be easy."

"No, sir. And frankly I'm hoping it won't come to that. I can't think of a worse fate now that I've met your daughter."

"She's so fragile," Laura muttered.

"She's stronger than we give her credit for, honey," her husband added.

Both of Ashley's parents stared at him for several moments, assessing his worth as though they could judge him by looking.

Laura finally spoke again. "You're welcome in our home any time. Please don't make me regret that decision."

"Of course, ma'am. And thank you."

"Tomorrow is Sunday. We usually have brunch at eleven if you'd like to join us," she added.

"That would be lovely. Thank you again." Evan stood. "I appreciate your candor. I'll let you folks get to bed. I'll be back in the morning." He headed for the door. He hadn't taken his coat off and he hadn't had a single sip of the coffee that sat on the table in front of him.

He needed to get out of there before he lost his mind breathing in his mate's scent. Even though she shared the home with her parents, her smell permeated every crevasse.

With a nod at the people he hoped would be his future in-laws, he left, closing the door behind him and jogging toward his car. Leaving his mate like this time and again was going to be the death of him. But it couldn't be helped.

~

Ashley paced her bedroom, trying to listen to the conversation going on in the living room. She couldn't hear much, but it sounded civil. No way in hell could she simply go to bed and fall asleep. Her heart was beating out of her chest, her hands were sweating profusely, and her libido had taken a sharp jump on the Richter scale.

No matter how hard she tried to prevent her body's reaction to Evan, it was useless. For the millionth time, she berated herself for ever being so weak as to stay with Damon for so long. It had never been more obvious than it was now that he was never her mate. He'd insisted he was, but he'd lied.

She'd been over this with her counselor so many times, but she still beat herself up wondering why she hadn't walked away from him. Especially in the last few years when he'd gotten lax and simply left her alone in the apartment. She could have walked out the door any day and never turned back. Why? Because of some babble about something called Stockholm Syndrome.

If she had, she wouldn't be as damaged as she viewed herself now.

She heard the front door shut and assumed Evan had left. Exhaling, partially in relief and partially in despair, she flopped down on her bed and hugged her pillow to her chest. She curled her knees underneath her and tucked them into her skirt. Any time she was stressed she reverted to this tight ball to escape life. She'd done it for years with Damon and she still did it whenever anxiety struck.

She could hear Dr. Parman's words ringing in her head from countless sessions. *"You are not to blame... You are the victim... You did nothing to provoke Damon's behavior."*

At the encouragement of Dr. Parman, Ashley had done her own research on other women who had gone through similar ordeals. Women taken from their lives and forced to obey their captor for years until they were rescued. Brainwashed. All of them. Beaten down until they felt they had no alternative but to stay.

Besides the physical abuse, nearly every victim of such a crime, Ashley included, had endured tremendous psychological abuse—nouns and verbs that forced them to question their self-worth, repeated badgering that led them to believe they deserved what they'd received, and threats made to harm their family and friends should they try to escape.

Intellectually, she had come to understand why everything happened the way it had, but deep inside she might never feel quite worthy of love or companionship from anyone, especially not someone claiming to be her mate.

Not that there was any doubt. Evan was clearly her mate.

Tears leaked down her face. Why couldn't she have met him before Damon? Why now?

She couldn't stand for anyone to touch her, even after six months of therapy. Even her own mother made her flinch.

How could she ever enter into a normal relationship with a man?

A knock sounded at the door. "Ashley?" The muffled voice of her mother reached through the door to soothe her. A moment later, the door creaked open and her mother stepped inside. "You okay?"

No. I'll never be okay.

She couldn't bring herself to tell her parents that though. They were hurting at least as much as she was. They went to counseling almost as often. They would forever beat themselves up for not finding her sooner, trusting their instincts, rescuing their only daughter.

Instead of opening wide the line of communication with her mother, Ashley chose to keep most thoughts to herself. She was broken enough as it was. There was no need to drag her mother down with her.

So she put forth a strong fake front most days, smiling and insisting she was doing fantastic, when really inside she was a ball of nerves with the nightmares to prove it.

"Evan seems nice," her mother said as she took a seat on the edge of the bed. The mattress dipped, but Ashley's mother didn't set a hand on her. She knew by now that any contact with her daughter had to be initiated by Ashley.

She hated that about herself. But direct contact with anyone made her flinch involuntarily every time, no matter who it was.

It was amazing she had allowed Evan to take her arm and guide her toward his car earlier. Perhaps the layers of clothing and coat had provided enough protection to help her disassociate from what was really happening. Someone had been protective, caring, thoughtful.

She didn't do those emotions these days. She didn't trust.

"Yeah."

"He's coming for brunch tomorrow."

Of course he is.

"Just... I won't tell you what to do." Her mother's tone was gentle.

"Thanks, Mom."

Instead of speaking another word, her mother reached for the comforter at the end of the bed and laid it over Ashley, and then she silently left the room.

CHAPTER 7

Evan pulled into his garage and set his forehead against the steering wheel. He hadn't stopped breathing rapidly since he left Ashley at her parents.

This wasn't how mating worked. It was nearly unheard of for mates to separate after meeting. It was bad enough he'd gone half a year knowing about Ashley, but now that he'd been in a confined space with her, the game had changed.

He needed her like he needed his next breath.

Instead he hauled himself into the house, dropped his keys on the table, and took off his coat. He was tired. Exhausted, more mentally than physically.

Ignoring his rock-hard cock, he crossed the room and turned on the coffee pot. All his nights went like this. He hadn't slept well since locating Ashley. His routine always started with a pot of coffee.

A flashing light to his left drew his attention to the answering machine. He pressed the button and listened to the only message with a smile.

"Evan? You okay? I'm worried about you. I had intended to ask you to start hunting for Parkfield for us again." Evan chuckled at the machine. "Guess that would be rather inappropriate under the circumstances. Call me." Josh. Of course. He'd avoided the man for weeks and now the cat was out of the bag. If Josh only knew the truth...

At least Josh wasn't angry. It wasn't as though this mating were something Evan controlled. It was the nature of shifters. It just happened. Nature didn't take convenience or timing into account.

Evan erased the message and turned back toward the coffee. He watched it drip into the pot, mesmerized by the steady slow stream of liquid that started out dark and turned gradually lighter.

He gripped the edge of the counter and tipped his head back to look at the ceiling. From one beat to the next, he made a decision. Ignoring the last slow drips falling into the pot, Evan grabbed his coat, stuffed his arms back inside, and swiped the keys off the counter.

Why hadn't he thought of this earlier?

In minutes he was speeding down the highway toward his favorite spot on earth. He didn't breathe fully until he'd parked the car in a thick patch of trees and exited. He shed his coat, dropping it on the front seat, followed by the rest of his clothes. It was cold, but he barely noticed. He only needed seconds.

On a deep breath, he shifted. Almost before his front paws hit the ground, he took off running. He sped between the trees, jumping over any obstacle, bounding as fast as he could to combat the stress he lived with daily.

Stress that had increased incrementally in the last few hours. It had been a risk, outing himself. He'd lived with the pain of knowing Ashley was his for months, but somehow keeping that information to himself had been less scary than sharing the details with the entire world.

Now he had a new set of problems. What if she turned him down? And more important, what if she didn't?

She brought a closet of skeletons he'd never fully understand. Sure, he'd researched the stresses Ashley would be facing after her return, but he had no way to comprehend the depth of her pain and suffering.

He was afraid he'd never be able to give her what she would need.

In the end, the best course of action might be to walk away, but he couldn't bring himself to do that without at least trying. He owed it to himself, and to her.

Evan ran hard. He pushed himself more than usual. He'd shifted more lately than ever before, finding that the only way to relieve even a small piece of his stress was to take off through the trees at a breakneck pace. The workouts did nothing to his libido, but at least he managed to sleep hard the few hours a night he allowed himself to slide between the sheets.

He was restless. Every time he lay down he dreamed of Ashley, his imagination running wild with whatever his mind conjured she might be like. If he'd had every one of those dreams written in a diary, they would fill several volumes and still not do justice to what he assumed a true claiming would be like.

He hadn't slept with another woman, shifter or human, since meeting Ashley. That hadn't slowed him down in the orgasm department. He masturbated to visions of Ashley daily, often more than once. Usually in the shower.

Evan stopped running and skidded to a halt when he reached his car. He hadn't realized he was back where he'd started until he'd nearly collided with the vehicle. He'd grown so accustomed to his route, he hadn't thought about his location while he ran.

Heaving for oxygen, Evan lay down on the ground next to his car and rested. If he'd been in human form, he'd have been sweating so hard, he'd be freezing. But in wolf form, he could only pant. He lay on the gravel and cocked his head toward the moon and the stars while he waited for his labored breathing to slow.

When he could delay no longer, and found himself chilly even in his fur, he shifted, yanked open the car door, and jerked all his clothes back on, heedless of whether or not they were straight, backward, or right-side out.

The car warmed rapidly as Evan rubbed his freezing hands on his jeans and waited for the windshield to clear.

God, she was gorgeous. He closed his eyes. The memory he'd had of her undernourished frame, her lank hair, and her deep sad eyes had been shattered by the woman he'd seen tonight. She'd put on weight. She was still skinny, but healthy. Her eyes glowed brighter, a green he could get lost in. And her hair had shown in the light.

Her smile, when she allowed herself to release it, brought tingles to his palms. He wanted to see that expression on her face more. Maybe it would erase some of the destruction.

Oh, who the hell was he kidding? He didn't know if she could ever overcome what she'd been through, and he had no idea if he was capable of rising to the task of her knight in shining armor.

~

Twenty minutes later, Evan was back at home. His coffee pot still sported the tiny orange light in the corner, indicating it had yet to time out and shut off. It would still be hot.

He grabbed a mug, filled it, and sauntered down the hall. At the first door on the left he paused. He stared hard at the dark wood finish, wishing what lay beyond had never existed. But as had been his custom for months, he turned the knob, took a deep breath, and entered the spare bedroom. There was no bed. Hell, there wasn't a dresser or a desk. Nope. The room's only contents were two massive folding tables and a spread of paper that would put the police department to shame.

It was time to work. It was late, later than he usually started working. He hoped he could sleep soon, but until his eyes drooped to the point of no return, he didn't dare go to his bedroom. The only thing worse than perpetual insomnia was falling asleep only to wake up an hour later covered in sweat, panting as though Evan himself had been the one kidnapped four years ago instead of Ashley.

Evan set his coffee cup on the corner of the table and laid his hand on the piece of paper he'd been perusing before sleep had claimed him last night. The room would look haphazard to anyone who saw it, not that anyone had, but to Evan it was organized chaos. He knew every single slip of paper, where it was located, and when he'd written on it.

This was not his office. Another bedroom across the hall contained the items of a real office—desk, fax machine, computer, filing cabinet. This room was special. This room had everything he needed to investigate one single case.

Damon Parkfield.

Unlike every night for as long as he could remember, Evan couldn't bring himself to sit on the only folding chair in the room. He didn't keep a nice sturdy desk chair in this room. He preferred to maintain a certain level of discomfort when dealing with the whereabouts of Mr. Parkfield. The bastard rankled him.

No one was paying Evan to continue looking for Damon. Josh mentioned on the answering machine he'd considered it. But the truth was, no one knew about his obsession. Evan was determined to bring to justice the man who called himself a member of the shifter community and had terrorized the woman Evan was fated to love.

Even though the elders of the wolf shifter community were investigating Damon and working hard to find him, Evan couldn't let it stop there. He wanted—no, *needed*—to make sure the bastard was brought to justice fast. He couldn't rest until then.

Evan smoothed his fingers across the table. He didn't have it in him tonight. His shoulders slumped. Perhaps it was the breakneck run, or the stress of having seen Ashley face-to-face tonight, but he was exhausted.

He stared at the unfinished coffee and left it sitting there as he backed out of the room and shut the door behind him.

Sleep. Was there a chance he could actually slumber peacefully finally?

Too tired for anything else, Evan used the bathroom that adjoined his room and brushed his teeth. He dropped his clothes in a line on the way to his bed and climbed between the sheets naked. He always slept naked. He preferred the feel of the silk against his skin to the confinement of boxers.

He closed his eyes and steadied his breathing.

Ashley.

~

Dark blonde hair danced along his chest, its owner's face curtained by the thick locks as the woman licked a trail across his pecs and then flicked her tongue over his nipple.

Evan moaned. He arched his back into the sensations tickling across his chest.

When she continued down his stomach, he gasped. Her

chin bumped into his cock as she swirled her tongue around his belly button. He grasped his thick shaft in one hand, unable to tolerate the torture of her sweet mouth on him, teasing him with promises of more. Instead of lowering her mouth to take his cock into her warmth, she nibbled her way back up to suck his nipples.

Her tiny moans filled the room.

He pumped his length harder, unable to stop himself with her scent filling his nostrils, her hair dangling across his chest, her soft lips torturing his skin. Her fingers danced across his chest, molding and sculpting his muscles as she kissed him.

With a loud groan, Evan came, pulsing against his stomach with more force than he ever remembered an orgasm having in the past. For a moment he lay there, relishing the experience with his mate...

His eyes shot open. He gasped into the darkness of the night. There was no Ashley. There was no sweet set of lips on his chest. Just blackness. Although he swore he could smell her lingering scent as though she'd been there.

Oh God. He had it bad.

CHAPTER 8

Ashley's entire body was on fire. Her heart wouldn't stop pounding at a rate that threatened to explode out of her chest. Every cell was alive and sensitive.

She'd uncurled from the tight ball at some point, stripped off her clothes, and climbed between the covers of the bed, hoping the cool sheets would bring her temperature down. She'd never been so hot. For years she'd been cold. She spent many nights in a damp basement or dark unfurnished spare rooms with no covers. She'd learned to wrap herself in a ball and hug her knees to her chest to stay warm.

Even after she'd come back home, she still rarely got between the sheets. Being covered was too confining. It made her feel trapped and afraid she couldn't get away fast enough. She always covered up with a throw blanket these days, but usually on top of the bed. Like she had tonight, before she'd started losing her mind.

In her bra and panties, she stretched out on the mattress. Her mind provided her with only one image—

Evan. She'd pictured him in many different scenarios, some imagined, some real. She couldn't shake him from her head. And she couldn't sleep either.

Her bra felt too tight, her nipples abrading against the cups. She tried to ignore it but eventually unclasped the confining lingerie and tossed it aside.

Well, that didn't help. Now her breasts rubbed the sheets. She set her hands across her belly in attempt to tent the cotton away from her chest.

Her nipples pebbled anyway, as though she were cold instead of burning up.

Maybe she had a fever.

Or maybe it was true what they said—*once a shifter meets their mate, there is no turning back.*

She groaned. No. No no no. She wasn't ready for this. She didn't think she'd ever be ready. But certainly not now. She wasn't whole. She wouldn't wish that on another being.

When a tingling started in her pussy, she spread her legs a few inches, hoping if she didn't rub them together, her clit wouldn't demand attention.

Again. All useless wishfulness.

Breathe. Eyes wide, she stared at the ceiling.

Evan Harmon. He was a big guy. And he was a PI. Maybe he could keep her safe if she gave him a chance. Or maybe she'd drag him down her path of destruction, endangering his life by having met her.

Ashley squeezed her eyes shut against the pain she felt, for herself and for everyone around her. The stress of her burden seemed insurmountable in the dark.

And here she lay, for the next six hours at least,

trying to keep anything from touching her skin and torturing her with the contact.

∼

Ashley leaned back in the armchair she'd chosen in her parents' basement den. She pulled her knees up to her chest in her usual stance.

She didn't move any more than necessary, but she let her gaze follow Evan as he wandered around the room admiring her mother's collection of porcelain angels.

It would have been comical and she would have laughed outright at his feigned interest, had she not been so terrified.

Brunch had been fine. Pleasant. *Okay, maybe possible is a better way to put it.*

Her parents had made small talk and she'd learned a lot about Evan and his work, where he lived, how long he'd been there, what his hobbies were...

Now they'd been banished to the den to "get to know each other."

Suddenly he turned and leaned against the far wall, crossing his legs at the ankles and his arms across his chest. He narrowed his gaze at her. "I'm sorry. I know you're uncomfortable. I want you to know I didn't plan this."

In a way he had. He could have kept this secret to himself forever, taken it to the grave.

She realized that was unfair, but under the circumstances she wasn't feeling generous.

She swallowed and licked her dry lips. "I don't know

what to say." *All my thoughts are jumbled and scattered and...mean.*

Her body warred with her mind. Ever since he'd arrived she'd had the urge to wrap her arms around his middle, squeeze him tight, feel his warmth, relax. Instead, she'd managed to distance herself and stay on edge.

She couldn't decide if she was teetering at the top of a mountain peak, trying desperately to avoid falling, or if she had actually already fallen and was in a free spin, flailing toward the ground.

Either way, she wished she could control her body's reaction to this man. Her palms sweated, her face flushed, her nipples wouldn't stop poking into her bra.

"I know I make you uncomfortable and that's to be expected, I guess. You've been through hell. It seemed prudent for me to leave you alone for as long as possible, and perhaps it's selfish of me to come forward even now, but it also would be unfair of me to keep our connection to myself and not give you the opportunity to tell me to take a hike." He grinned.

"It's not you. I'm...empty inside. Not whole. I don't know when or if I'll ever be normal again. It would be unfair of *me* to keep you on a leash tethered to a woman who may or may not ever be able to look you in the eye."

"I'm only asking you to give me a chance. You don't know me. Maybe I'm a good guy. Maybe I can rise to the challenge and be your everything."

"Maybe I will destroy your faith and make your life a living hell." She cringed.

"I doubt that. I'm tough." He approached her slowly.

She shook, her arms and legs stiff and tight as he knelt in front of her. In this position, his face was lower than hers and he looked up at her with pleading eyes.

Shocking herself, she unleashed one arm from around her knees and grazed a finger across his cheekbone. So firm and masculine. Warm.

He lifted his own hand, encompassed her small one in his larger one, and tipped his head sideways to snuggle into her touch.

Her mouth went dry. *Holy mother of God*. She froze. Her eyes wouldn't close to blink. She stared into his unwavering gaze and drank him in. As though the contact united them in some ancient way of wolves, she struggled to breathe. Her world tipped on its axis, making her dizzy. She released her grip around her knees and leaned forward until their faces were mere inches apart. Her body calmed and warmed and came alive all at the same time.

Her breath mingled with his, and she shifted her gaze to his lips. What would they feel like? With the hand he held against his cheek, she reached her thumb out to stroke across his lower lip. He gasped and she smiled inwardly at her ability to affect him. Thank God she wasn't alone in this.

Ashley reached with her free hand to set it on his chest. The resistance of his rock-hard pecs made her shiver. She'd never intentionally touched Damon's chest, but he didn't work out. She'd always thought him soft and scrawny. Evan was everything Damon would never be.

Large, foreboding. Hard. A gentle giant. Kind.

Again she wished she had met him five years ago instead of yesterday. Her life would have been so normal, not filled with pain and suffering.

Evan reached tentatively with his free hand toward her face. He swiped his thumb across her cheek, catching a tear she hadn't known had escaped from her eye. His sensitivity astounded her. Her body came alive under his touch. Her jeans felt tight and rubbed against her pussy, stifling the folds of her sex and squishing her clit under its hood.

Ashley squeezed her legs together, closed her eyes, and inhaled long and deep the scent of her mate. It felt so right.

And then he scooted closer and she opened her eyes to gaze at him once more. Lust darkened his chocolate eyes to a deeper shade, almost black.

She panicked. Fear flooding her system as she shuffled away from him with both feet, jerking her hands from his grip and his shirt, leaning back in the chair as though the air there might not be as thin.

She heaved a deep breath. "I can't do this." She knew her eyes were wide with fear.

Evan sat back on his heels and set his hands on his knees. "It's okay," he murmured, smiling at her.

"No. Really. It's not." She shook her head, gripped the arms of the chair so tight her fingers ached.

"I didn't mean to pressure you." He stood and took a step back. "I'm sorry."

"No. I'm sorry. Sorry Fate dragged you into my nightmare. This isn't fair to you. You should go. Find a woman who will make a better mate. Someone whole. Someone not damaged." She fought the tears that welled up in the corners of her eyes. *Do not cry.*

"Oh, baby, you are so much more than damaged and unwhole. You just need more time to work through years of abuse." He rubbed his neck as he spoke, clearly uncomfortable.

She shook her head. "Please, just go. I'm not ready for this. It's too overwhelming. I can't face mating anyone. It's not on my long list of things to do and that list is very long. Please. Let it be. I understand it'll be hard, but the less time we spend together, the easier it will be to separate. Find another mate. Claim someone else and forget about me." She ducked her head, letting her hair fall around her face, hoping it would hide her feelings, her emotions, her…self.

Evan stood and backed away. She didn't look up, but she sensed his distance as it grew with each step. It hurt. Her chest felt like it was being crushed by weights. Each step he took increased the pressure. *You told him to go. Insisted.*

She breathed shallowly, not wanting to miss a moment of his presence. She'd never feel again in her life what she'd felt for the two minutes she'd stared into his eyes. His scent would linger in the room, but it would dissipate over time.

She needed to hold strong. She was no good for him. He was a nice man. He deserved better than what she could ever offer under the best of scenarios.

The door to the basement snicked shut as he disappeared at the top of the steps. She jumped in her seat, lifted her face. He was gone. She sucked in a lungful of oxygen and let the tears fall down her face. A sob escaped.

It was for the best. She knew that. But it still hurt. And the pain would linger for a long time.

CHAPTER 9

Two months later...

"Evan? Where are you? I've been trying to reach you forever." Josh sounded rushed and frantic through the phone. Was something wrong with Ashley?

"I had to leave town to follow a lead."

"Just like that? I thought you weren't traveling anymore. You left without a word. You've been gone for weeks."

"Listen, Josh. It was too hard. I couldn't stay in St. Louis. It's a big city, but not big enough for both Ashley and I to occupy if we're to deny our mating." He'd grown to agree with her, strengthening his resolve each day. She was right. It would be impossible to try and make something work between them. There were other fish in the sea. He'd find one…eventually.

Josh took a deep breath. "You don't seriously believe you can walk away, do you?"

"She gave me no choice."

"She's confused," Josh shouted. "And this isn't helping. Now she's worse."

Evan sank down onto the mattress of his hotel room, his shoulders slumping. He didn't need to hear all that.

"Please, come home. Come over and we can talk. She needs you, even if she won't admit it."

"I can't right now. I'm in the middle of a case." Never mind he was chasing his tail trying to locate Damon Parkfield. And never mind every lead he followed up on led to nowhere. Whatever that bastard was up to, Evan grew more impatient with each passing day.

If he couldn't be with Ashley, the least he could do was spend his days seeking justice on her behalf.

"Why do I think there's something you aren't telling me?"

Evan squeezed his eyes shut. *Because there are lots of things I'm not telling you, and you're a smart guy.*

"You're hunting that bastard, aren't you?"

"Who are you talking about? I'm always hunting a bastard."

"Sure. But this time you're chasing Ashley's ex. Don't fuck with me, man. Stop it and come home. The Head Council is working on it. You don't need to make this your mission."

Yeah. The elders at The Head Council were working on the case. It was in their hands, at least. But, they weren't doing anything fast enough as far as Evan was concerned.

It didn't matter if Ashley never spoke to Evan again.

Even if she was never able to mate and hold a normal relationship, she still deserved vengeance. And Evan knew she wouldn't rest easy until her ex was caught.

"Evan, I can hear your mind spinning. This is madness. You could get hurt. We don't know what that asshole is capable of. What if you do find him? What are you going to do? Shoot him? How will that help Ashley? You're useless to her from jail."

To be honest, Evan didn't know what he planned to do with Damon when he found him. He only knew his mind was on one track and that was locating the bastard. "I'm fine. Don't worry about me. I have an appointment tomorrow and then I'll come home for a few days. Maybe we can get together if I'm not too busy." He had no intention of seeing Josh this week, but if saying so made the guy simmer down, he'd play along.

"I'm worried about you. Please be careful. Call me when you get here. If I don't hear from you in two days, I'm heading to your house. Got it?"

"Yep. No problem." *I won't be there, but you go right ahead.*

"'Kay. Later. Stay safe." Josh hung up. His last words hadn't been enthusiastic. He was leery and rightfully so.

Josh did have a valid point though. What was Evan going to do when he found Damon? He couldn't very well kill the guy and move on.

Evan hadn't been entirely untruthful. He did have a meeting tomorrow. He had a six o'clock flight to Seattle to meet with the elders of the North American Council. He wanted to follow up with them on what they'd found and ensure they were indeed making progress.

The elders knew who Evan was. His work wasn't a total secret. Hell, he'd done jobs for them in the past. The Council had hired him to find a few people over the years. And they were well aware of his involvement in finding Ashley in the first place eight months ago.

What they didn't realize was that Evan's life mission was tracking this bastard. And to be honest, Ashley wasn't his only motivation. The jackass had some mysterious drug on him and Evan wanted it found. He doubted the stupid fucker was making his own drugs, which meant he was acquiring the substance from someone else. Was the supplier a shifter?

Evan cringed. He couldn't stand the thought of a fellow wolf shifter making and distributing drugs, especially experimental drugs used to keep people malleable. How many others were being drugged?

Evan had spent countless hours, days, and weeks tracking other missing shifters. He'd interviewed numerous parents of recently mated couples to see if other young girls were unaccounted for. He wanted to know if there was anyone else out there under the influence of these drugs. It was grueling work because of the nature of their species. It wasn't uncommon for newly mated wolves to take off together. There could be any number of families out there who didn't realize their sister, daughter, or cousin was actually being drugged and held against her will rather than having been claimed voluntarily.

So far only one family seemed to believe with certainty that their daughter may also have been a victim. It was promising, but had led to nothing but dead ends. Allison Watkins. Her parents, Geoff and Holly, had only heard from her a few times since The Gathering nine months ago. They were worried and informed The Council at Evan's urging.

Where the hell was Allison? And why did her story sound eerily familiar?

Evan didn't believe Damon had snatched Allison because nine months ago he'd still been with Ashley. The chances he'd been involved were slim. The idea made Evan shake until he lay back against the mattress in attempt to relieve his muscles. Who took Allison then? And how widespread was this drug problem?

He closed his eyes and pictured the sweet face of Ashley behind his lids. He swallowed around the lump that formed in his throat every time he thought about her. He needed her. Perhaps more than he had before he'd confronted her. Did she suffer as much as him?

He was beginning to doubt the adage that time and distance would ease the pain. Each day his chest hurt worse and he lost more of his ability to concentrate on anything but her memory. If she'd been dead, that would have been another story. But his mate was alive and well, hiding out in her parents' home from a boogeyman Evan intended to catch.

~

Damon stuffed his duffle bag hastily for the umpteenth time in months. Years, really. Why couldn't he shake these bastards off his trail? He was careful. He always fled with nothing but what he could carry. He never left a trace as far as he was concerned. He took a bus most of the time to avoid using any identification.

Hell, he even used throw-away cell phones he smashed repeatedly and left behind with each move, ditching them in a public trash can.

"Motherfucking assholes," he muttered to himself. *If Ashley's damn family hadn't intervened, this never would have happened.* Why couldn't those fools have left well enough alone? If the bitch had ever gotten pregnant and produced some cubs for him, she'd have been much more inclined to stay by his side.

But no, Ashley had been stronger willed than he'd ever suspected when he'd first laid eyes on her. She'd fought him every step of the way and had never been the docile pleasant wench he'd been guaranteed the injections he'd given her would produce.

Now he was growing weary of all the moving around the country. It didn't matter a fuck that he received a regular allowance in exchange for keeping his fucking mouth shut. He was bone tired from being on alert, and now he didn't even have a woman in his life to take his aggravation out on.

If the fucking Romulus, his mysterious benefactor, didn't come up with a new, more-agreeable mate for him soon, he had every intention of breaking any deal they thought they had with him and going it alone. They had stolen almost five years of his life with their fucking promises and demands.

When they had first shown up at his doorstep five years ago with a grandiose plan to make his life a field in paradise, he'd jumped at the idea. With no living relatives and no mate, their proposition seemed sound enough. He'd been separated from all other wolf shifters for over a decade. Not that he'd been hiding. Just that he hadn't cared to attend the biennial Gathering and he'd lived quite far from any other shifters.

Damon zipped up the duffle with a jerk and stared at the second bag he carried everywhere he went. Maybe he should leave that motherfucking shit behind this time and make his own way in life. This particular existence wasn't panning out well.

Surely he could go it alone and drop the fucking Romulus and their damn secrets and sleep better at night.

He plopped onto the bed and leaned his elbows on his knees, burring his head in his hands. That plan wouldn't get him another mate, or return the one he had. Nope. He was fucking doomed to wait this out a little longer before he went rogue...more rogue than he already was.

After five years of working with these people, he still knew very little about them except they were very powerful with serious financial backing. Damon didn't live well, for fuck's sake, but he did live almost exclusively off the constant supply of money the Romulus sent him. Any odd jobs he managed to get in each location provided icing on the cake so he could enjoy life a bit.

Why they referred to themselves as the Romulus, he had no idea. He knew there were brothers, Romulus and Remus, in Roman mythology who were nursed by a wolf in infancy. It was a common story shifters learned as children. Many shifters believed Romulus and Remus were the predecessors of today's wolf-shifting community. Eventually Romulus killed his brother. If this group was called the Romulus, was there a Remus also? He cackled to himself. Except for the first time two men had come to his door years ago, he'd never met personally with any of them. He wouldn't be able to describe the individuals he'd initially met with if he tried. It had been so long.

One thing he did know, if he had it to do over again, he would never choose this path. It hadn't been worth it. He'd been promised a fucking mate and offspring to start his own pack of which he would be the Alpha. King. He was hanging on by a thread now with more promises the Romulus were going to make everything right, providing him with a new mate and guaranteeing him things would go better with her.

He sighed. At this point he couldn't decide if he was more pissed with the fucking Romulus for getting him into this nomad lifestyle, or that damn bitch Ashley for not complying with the game plan. No matter what involvement the Romulus had in his initial claiming of the bitch, she never respected him the way a mate should. His blood still boiled thinking about her fleeing him that day last year. Who the fuck did she think she was? She was his, damnit, and if he ever got the opportunity, he would remind her of this in no uncertain terms.

She would pay. The Romulus didn't need to know his thoughts on Ashley. Hell, lately any ideas he had concerning his wayward mate were about the only thing he still held sacred. The Romulus seemed to have eyes everywhere. They fucking called him so often with relocation instructions he could barely lie down in one bed for more than a week at a time.

Motherfucker.

It was time to go.

Backing through the small apartment, Damon glanced around in the usual manner, covering his bases as he had dozens of times in the past. He glanced out the window at the dead of night, verified no one was currently watching, and then slipped into the darkness and moved stealthily away from this latest existence in bum-fuck Indiana.

~

Ashley sat at her easel in the art studio her father had relegated to one half of the basement. It dawned on her she'd been holding her brush in the air for ages when her arm began to shake. A clean canvas rested in front of her but there was no paint on the brush. In fact, there was no paint on her pallet.

She relaxed her arm, shaking her head against her complete distraction. She couldn't think or concentrate anymore. It grew worse every day. Her thoughts were filled with one thing—Evan Harmon. She'd only seen him that one weekend, but his features were burned into the back of her eyelids. She knew his scent as though he were in the room with her. She could conjure it at will and would spin her head in every direction looking for him.

He was never there.

It was her own fault. She'd told him to leave. She'd asked him not to come back. She'd sent him away all by herself.

She knew he'd left town, buried himself in work. It was for the best.

Right?

Ugh.

Ashley set the paintbrush down and wandered to the window. It was gorgeous outside. Her parents had a walkout basement, so one side opened to the backyard. It had snowed all night and the ground was white, unadulterated by footprints this early in the day.

The world looked pristine and pure. Giant flakes drifted casually from the sky as though in no hurry to reach their destination.

She closed her eyes. Nothing about her life was as calm, relaxed, simple, or unpolluted as the backyard was. She felt as though she muddied the ground just by looking.

It was ridiculous of course, but the idea still seeped into her mind.

Footsteps on the stairs made her spin around. She almost tripped over her own feet, heart pounding as she waited for the owner of the stomping feet to emerge.

"Hey, squirt," Josh announced as his legs came into view.

She set her hand on her chest and glared in his direction.

"Sorry," he said when he noticed her stance. "I forgot

to announce myself." He strolled across the room and briefly pecked her cheek.

She couldn't ask for better family. Even her own brother took care of her.

"Why are you off today?"

"It's Monday. I'm always off on Mondays." He stepped toward her easel and furrowed his brow as he stared at the blank canvas. And then he chuckled and grinned at her. "I get it now. You're working on a rendition of the yard. Cute. You've nailed it."

"Ha ha." She tried to be miffed with his not-so-subtle jibe, but she couldn't hold the emotion. A smile crept across her face. "I'm good. What can I say?" She shrugged.

"You okay?" He wandered toward her.

"Yep." *No.*

"I spoke to Evan last night."

And you found it necessary to tell me this why? She bit the inside of her cheek to keep from saying anything. Who cared if Josh spoke to Evan?

He continued anyway. "He's got some meeting today and then he says he's coming home for a few days."

"So? How does this concern me?" She cross her arms and hugged herself tight, suddenly cold.

Josh fingered the afghan on the back of the couch and leaned his hip against the upholstery. "Don't try that with me, Ash. I mated with Samantha months ago myself. I know you have to be hurting, no matter what you say. I don't know how you can do it."

"Do what?" She dipped her head, sorry she'd asked.

"Ignore the calling."

Deflated, Ashley's shoulders fell. He was right. Every time she thought about Evan her heart pounded and her body reacted in ways she could barely define. Sure, she'd had sex. Obviously she'd had sex. But she'd never felt half what she felt just thinking about Evan. No encounter with Damon compared to the way her body reacted to Evan's the one and only time he'd touched her cheek for several brief seconds two months ago.

But then she considered the future. She would be a pain in his ass for life if she dragged him into her mess. It wasn't fair to him.

"Why are you doing this?"

"Doing what?" She knew good and well what he referred to, but it was so much easier to play ignorant.

"Pretending you don't care. Faking like you can brush Evan under the rug and move on."

"Any other choice would be cruel."

"And you think what you're doing isn't? You're only hurting both of you." He held up a hand when she stepped back. "Look, I didn't come here to lecture you. I'm sorry."

He circled the couch and took a seat. "How are your classes going?"

"Okay." She was taking two online classes this semester, trying to get her feet back under her. At least they occupied her mind and kept her busy. Her art filled the rest of her time, when she was able to disassociate and really let herself go long enough to concentrate.

"Just okay?"

"Stop acting like Mom and Dad. I get enough of that already."

Josh chuckled. "All right. Fine. You win. Listen, the reason I came by was to see if you wanted to go for a run."

Her heart pounded hearing the words. She was already shaking her head before he finished the sentence. "It's snowing outside. The weather sucks."

He laughed again. "Ash, you know good and well it's the perfect weather. No one would come upon us and it's beautiful. It's my favorite time to shift. And it's so rare to get to do so during the day."

"I have a lot to do." She ducked her head and stared at her feet, shuffling them on the floor. "I have homework and I'm working on a painting."

"The one with the snow scene?" He pointed to the easel, half his mouth lifted in a grin when she glanced up.

"Look, Josh. I'm not ready, okay? Stop pestering me. I can't do it. I don't want to. And I'm not going to."

He lifted both hands in surrender. "Okay. I'm just trying to help. I thought maybe if I went with you and we went during the day you might consider leaving the house."

"Not yet." She felt bad for raising her voice. It wasn't his fault she was such a wuss. "I'm working on it."

"I know you are, Ash." He leaned back and let his head fall against the back of the couch. He seemed to stare at the ceiling.

She knew he was disappointed, and he meant the best for her, but she couldn't be what everyone else wanted her to be. Healed. She eased closer and took a seat next to her brother. "It's so hard, knowing he's out there somewhere. I keep thinking he's lying in wait, hiding, waiting for the opportunity to jump out and grab me. I know it's unreasonable and he probably could care less if he ever saw me again, but that doesn't erase the fear."

"I know, Ash." He reached for her hand and she let him squeeze her fingers. "Have you heard from The Head Council lately? Do they have any leads on either him or the drugs?"

"Nope. Not a word. I'm sure they're working on it, and I doubt they want me hounding them all the time to follow up."

"I keep hoping they'll have a breakthrough soon," Josh added.

"I'm sure they have more important things to do than to track down a man who is no longer holding someone hostage. I heard there are other women presumed missing now."

Josh jerked his head up and his gaze to hers. "Where did you hear that?"

"Mom and Dad were discussing it. They didn't know I was listening." She narrowed her gaze at him. "You knew it too, didn't you?"

"Yeah, but I didn't want you to worry."

"Do you think it's Damon?"

Josh shook his head. "No. I think there are other cases that seem similar and may or may not be definitive leads. Please don't worry, okay?"

"Who said I was worried?" She smiled. She'd never been more worried in her life. If anyone out there was going through what she went through... She had the urge to vomit.

Josh stood. "I have to go. I'm meeting Nathan and Samantha for that run."

"They aren't working today?"

"They are. But we agreed to meet for a long lunch."

"And you thought it would be a good idea to drag me along as the third...er, fourth wheel? No thanks, bro. That sounds disgusting."

He kissed her forehead and headed for the stairs. "It wouldn't have been like that and you know it. I'm perfectly capable of acting respectable whenever necessary."

"But you're still relieved I said no on some level. Admit it."

"Never." She watched as he disappeared up the stairs. When he shut the door at the top, she turned to look out the window. The world was white, as white as her canvas. She prayed one day she'd be able to go outside again. She'd give anything to simply smell the outdoors without fear of detection.

She hadn't been born a hermit and she was stir-crazy. But not enough to risk going outside.

Dr. Parman said it was temporary and natural for her to suffer a certain level of agoraphobia after what she'd been through. As long as she didn't remain trapped in this state of mind forever, it was an acceptable part of her progress.

CHAPTER 10

Evan took a seat at the long conference table. He was the only person on his side of the table, directly across from the five men who made up the elders of the North American Council. He rubbed his hands on his khaki pants, the nicest clothing he had with him on this trip.

He'd spoken to various shifters who worked in this head branch office, but none of the five men sitting across from him now. In fact, he'd never met any of them before. At least not that he could recall. Perhaps as a child, but not in his adult years.

Evan hadn't been to The Gathering for many years. His parents, Roland and Veronica, had retired and moved to Florida four years ago. They'd hated the Midwest weather. He'd been an only child and hadn't attended The Gathering even when his parents were still living in St. Louis. School always seemed to have gotten in the way, or so he claimed. He'd been secretly uninterested in finding a mate at the time—and after all, that was one of the main reasons The Gathering occurred.

The council members all attended every year, but young shifters paid them no attention. The only thing the children were interested in was reacquainting with friends they saw once a year.

As the kids grew older, their only concern was flirting with the opposite sex in hopes of finding a match. It was ridiculous since very few wolves actually knew who their mates were before adulthood. Even the ones who crossed paths on occasion before turning eighteen rarely were aware of the plans Fate had for them. Most of the time mates didn't find each other until their twenties. It was part of Her design.

The man in the center spoke first. He was the oldest, at least seventy. His name was Ralph Jerard. Evan had looked up every member of The Council and studied their profiles before he headed to Seattle. Mr. Jerard wore glasses low on his nose when looking down at the file of papers in front of him. His hair was gray and his skin wrinkled with age, but he was not frail. He was still stocky and fit, not uncommon for wolf shifters. "We understand you've been working on the Damon Parkfield case."

"Yes, sir, I have. Is that a problem?" If the elders had dragged him here from Indiana to reprimand him for something he had no intention of changing, he was going to be pissed.

"No. On the contrary, we're hoping to combine our efforts since you seem intent on finding this rogue shifter and bringing him to justice." The elder leaned forward on his elbows and set his glasses on the table. "That is your intent, correct?" He narrowed his gaze.

Evan knew what this game was. Mr. Jerard wanted to ensure Evan didn't have an ulterior motive, such as murder. "Of course, sir." He didn't break eye contact.

"You're a private investigator, correct?"

"Yes, sir."

"And you're the same PI who located Ms. Rice several months ago and returned her to her family?"

"That's correct. Her brother hired me when he suspected foul play. It took almost a year to track them down. If I'd had any idea at the time how serious the crime was, I never would have walked away that day after rescuing Ashley from the apartment they were living in."

"And where is Ashley Rice now?" Mr. Jerard asked.

"At her parent's home. She suffers from PTSD. She doesn't leave the house often."

"I see. And where do you believe Damon Parkfield is now?"

"I tracked him to a small town in Indiana last week, but he disappeared before I got there, as usual. It's very frustrating how fast he catches on to me. Either he has incredible luck and happens to move around at a pace one step ahead of mine, or someone is alerting him to my arrival." Evan shivered at the verbalization of that thought.

"Is that possible?"

"No." Evan shook his head. "Because no one knows I'm working on this case. Not a soul." He paused. "With the exception of you, of course. He usually rents a run-down furnished apartment and flees quickly. I don't know what tips him off or if he just likes to move around often. He doesn't strike me as being someone who could accomplish all this on his own. Someone must be funding him. He never holds a job very long and hasn't worked anywhere that would pay the rent for ages."

"Do you believe he's traveling alone?" Mr. Jerard asked.

"I do. Every time I enter his latest location I rummage around looking for clues. I have seen no evidence he has anyone with him at this time. So, if you're asking me if I think he has another woman with him, the answer is no." Evan had meticulously gone through the man's trash at every location. He'd seen nothing to indicate Damon had taken another woman.

"Well, that's good."

"Unless of course you take a long look at the list of parents who have very little or similar contact with their young daughters as Ashley Rice's family did—and I'm sure you all have done that. In which case you have no choice to but assume this problem extends way beyond Damon Parkfield and could in fact be a conspiracy of huge proportions."

"We wondered if that had occurred to you." Mr. Jerard looked back and forth at the other men with him. He lifted his papers and tapped them on the table to straighten the stack.

"Gentleman, you can stop ignoring the elephant in the room. I'm painfully aware there is undoubtedly a black market of some sort distributing a new drug concoction whose purpose is to keep its victim docile and controllable. The question is why? Who is making the drugs? And how widespread is the distribution?" Evan saw no reason to skirt this issue another moment. If these men had called him to Seattle to meet with them—all five of them—then they had an agenda and he intended to get to the bottom of it as soon as possible.

The man to the left of Mr. Jerard leaned to the side to whisper something in the older man's ear.

Evan had excellent hearing, but then so did every other shifter in the room. It made whispering at a lower decibel necessary for them all. He couldn't make out a single word.

Evan glanced at the other men at the table. The elderly man to the right of Mr. Jerard was Melvin Cunningham. His narrowed gaze made Evan nervous. Mr. Cunningham leaned back in his chair and tapped his cheek with two fingers, never removing his gaze from Evan. The two men flanking the group on both ends were Earl Johnson and Lucas Sheffield. Both were middle aged.

Finally, the taller, skinnier man on the left, who Evan knew was Steven Wightman, cleared his throat and sat straight. "Who has been paying you for your work so far, sir?"

"No one." That was the truth. Evan hadn't received a dime for his efforts. The only way he'd stayed afloat financially was by expanding his company and hiring others to work for him. Somehow he'd managed to stay in the black. But he knew he couldn't keep it up much longer. It was expensive traveling all around the country chasing his tail.

"Why?" Mr. Wightman asked.

"Sir?"

"What reason do you have to follow a convict from state to state for no financial gain?" Mr. Wightman held Evan's gaze.

In fact, Evan could feel all eyes piercing him. Though the other three men hadn't said a word during this meeting, they were paying close attention. There was no reason to lie. He'd eventually be found out anyway. "Ms. Rice is my mate."

No one flinched. He hadn't shocked them.

Mr. Jerard spoke again. "And you believe you can remain impartial in this case with the victim as your mate?"

Evan shook his head. "I never said I was impartial. I intend to find Damon Parkfield and bring him to justice. If you're asking me if I'm planning to shoot the man in the skull and ask questions later, the answer is no. I want him alive as much as you do. It's the only way to get information from him about who his supplier is and catch the real bad guy.

"Until Mr. Parkfield is apprehended, Ashley Rice's life is on hold. She's frozen with fear. Yes, she's my mate. However, you need to know she has not allowed me to claim her. No action has been taken to make her mine. In fact, I've only met with her on two short occasions since her rescue, both of those recent. She's in no position to be claimed. Nor does she have any interest."

"And you believe if you can find Damon Parkfield and get him off the streets, Ms. Rice will accept you?" Mr. Wightman asked.

Evan shook his head. "Not at all. There are no guarantees she will ever be able to move on with her life. However, it's a step in the right direction, and it gives me something useful to do rather than sit around pining and waiting."

"Fair enough." Mr. Wightman leaned in to whisper something in Mr. Jerard's ear again. When he sat back, he continued. "Would you give us a moment to confer?"

"Of course." Evan stood abruptly, almost tipping his chair over backward. He straightened his shirt and turned to leave the room. As soon as the door snicked shut behind him, he took a seat on the plush chair in the hall.

A few people wandered past while he waited. None of them spoke, but they all nodded cordially and smiled. They must have thought he was in serious trouble to be waiting outside what was obviously the regular chambers of The Head Council's main group of elders.

After several minutes, the door opened next to him and one of the younger elders who had flanked the right side of the group, Lucas Sheffield, leaned his head out. "Please. Come back in."

Evan reentered the room and resumed his seat across from The Council when the younger man motioned toward the chair.

Once they were all seated again, Mr. Jerard spoke. "While the five of us admit we have some serious concerns with regard to your relationship with Ashley

Rice, we are impressed with the work you've done and find you to be truthful and forward with your admissions. We believe it's in the best interest of The Council, yourself, and Ms. Rice for us to retain your services toward the goal of apprehending Mr. Parkfield and bringing him in for questioning.

"Would you be agreeable to joining our payroll toward that end?" Mr. Jerard asked the question, but Evan didn't get the sense it was really a question. It was more of a demand. The elders could be very persuasive if push came to shove and this issue necessitated extreme measures.

"I would be honored, sir." Evan nodded. He'd been completely in the dark about The Council's reasons for calling him in. Anything had been possible from reprimanding him for sticking his nose into the case to coercing him to give up all the information he had acquired thus far. Until Mr. Jerard had insinuated their interest in hiring him, that possibility hadn't been on his radar.

This arrangement would solve a lot of problems, the most important of which was Evan's financial situation.

"Good. We need you to sign a confidentiality agreement and then we'll hand over everything we have on this case. Please use the utmost discretion when dealing with any issue concerning the apprehension of Mr. Parkfield and the confiscation of any drug paraphernalia. We don't want to cause widespread paranoia, nor do we want anyone outside of this room to be informed about any aspect of this case. Is that agreeable to you?" Mr. Jerard asked. His eyes never moved from Evan's as he spoke. The man didn't appear to blink.

"Of course, sir. You have my word." But why so secretive that the other twenty individuals who worked at The Head Council weren't privy to any information? Wouldn't it have been beneficial to everyone if more hands, eyes, and ears were on deck?

And then it dawned on Evan. He raised his eyebrows and glanced at every man behind the long conference table. "You think it's someone inside."

Mr. Wightman tipped his head toward the table as he answered. "We don't know that for certain, Mr. Harmon. But, yes. It's a suspicion. We don't want to take any chances."

"Can you start immediately?" Mr. Jerard asked without elaborating.

"Yes. But I'd like a day to return to St. Louis if you don't mind."

The elders collectively stood as Mr. Jerard addressed the request. "We're okay with that as long as it doesn't interfere with the case in any way. We cannot emphasize enough the need to not jeopardize the research we have collected so far."

He stepped around the table as he continued. "I'm sure you have a mountain of your own information regarding this investigation. That's the main reason we want to hire you. It was only recently that we discovered the probable depth of this criminal activity. We'd like that to remain between the six of us, and seeing as you aren't a man to be stopped in your own exploration of the case, we might as well bring you in to join the team.

"It's our hope that by combining our research with yours, you will have a stronger case and be armed with the ability to track Mr. Parkfield with all haste."

"I will do my best, sir." Evan extended his hand as Mr. Jerard did. His shake was firm. The man's piercing gray eyes were menacing, almost threatening as he portrayed the seriousness of this matter with a single glance.

"Mr. Wightman will escort you to human resources to sign some forms. You may return to St. Louis today. We've already purchased you a ticket on the next flight." Mr. Jerard reached into his inner suit pocket and pulled out an envelope. He handed it to Evan as he continued. "There is a retainer check inside as well. Take today to look in on your loved ones and we will arrange for our research to arrive at your house tomorrow. We expect it will take you several days, or even a week to go through everything and combine our work with your own. Take whatever time you need before you travel again.

"We only ask that you remain in contact with us daily by phone or email and keep us abreast of the situation."

Evan nodded. Somehow in the last half hour the seriousness of this case rose to a new height. He intended to get to the bottom of it if it was the last thing he did. He owed that much to Ashley and to any other woman out there who might be involved in a similar predicament.

A chill went down Evan's spine as he followed Mr. Wightman down the hall. How many women? He pictured girls barely out of their teens, girls like Ashley, abused and held against their will. Drugged into submission by wolf shifters who insisted they were their mates.

Why? What was the motive?

Evan had no idea, but he intended to find out.

CHAPTER 11

Ashley set her paintbrush down and stared at the canvas in front of her. What was she painting? She'd meant to do a snowy day after staring out the window and talking to her brother, but whatever she'd created on that blank canvas was anything but snow. She hadn't even used any white. It looked chaotic. And it represented what she imagined the inside of her brain looked like today.

Every day was a stressful day since the confrontation with Evan, but she usually kept her feelings at bay by ignoring them. After Josh left, she'd been bombarded with thoughts she'd have preferred not to entertain.

Her muscles ached from the stiff brush strokes. Even her neck and her back rebelled when she tried to pop her head from side to side.

Giving up, she headed upstairs.

During the day, her mother usually left her alone.

She'd taken to hiding in the basement studying or painting and she'd made it clear she hated being disturbed. She knew she was hiding from far more than her parents and life. She was hiding from herself. And she was hiding from the reality she'd chosen not to accept.

"Hey, honey. Did you get a painting finished today?"

Ashley smirked. "You could say that. Though I doubt it's going to sell at a famous gallery and set me for life." She reached into the refrigerator for a bottle of water.

Her mother smiled as she looked up from where she chopped vegetables at the kitchen island. "I love all your work."

"That's great, Mom." Ashley shook her head and leaned against the island, trying not to sound too sarcastic. It wasn't her mother's fault. Nothing was. Though she knew her parents felt intense guilt for not doing more to prevent the four years of torture she'd undergone.

"Did anyone call?" *Now why did I have to go and ask that?* She never questioned her mother on such things. She didn't want to hear the answers.

Her mother lifted her gaze and set her knife down. "Yes." She paused. "He calls every day, Ash."

Really? She hadn't realized that. Her heart started racing and she stood upright. "You never mentioned that," she mumbled.

"You made it pretty clear you didn't want to hear about it."

That was true. But every day? "What does he say?"

"He asks how you're doing and if we need anything.

He's the nicest man I've ever met to be honest, after your father, of course." Her mother smiled.

"Does he ask to speak to me?"

"No."

Ashley's chest deflated at that one word, though she had no idea why.

Suddenly she felt antsy. She needed to move. Her entire body came alive as she pictured Evan calling her mother every day to see if Ashley was okay.

She turned on her heel and fled the room, nearly jogging to her bedroom. When she entered, she shut the door behind her and locked it. She paced the floor, unable to move fast enough or far enough in the cramped space.

What she needed was to run off some steam in wolf form. She stopped at the window and grabbed the frame with both hands, squeezing until her knuckles hurt. The snow fell harder now than it had earlier. It drifted at a steady pace toward the ground, blanketing the world in white. Not a blade of grass or a stray leaf remained visible.

It would feel so good beneath her feet. But she wasn't ready. Just imagining opening the window made her heart skip a beat. No. She couldn't do it. And besides, a run of a hundred miles wouldn't erase her thoughts of Evan.

What if she went to see him tomorrow? Josh had said he would be in town for the day. Maybe she could talk to him and ask him to stop calling. That would help rid her system of him.

She groaned, knowing she was lying to herself. Her

knees threatened to buckle and she turned around, leaned her back against the wall under the window, and slid down to the floor.

She tucked her knees up against her chest and hugged them, her chin on her kneecaps.

Ashley closed her eyes, but all she could picture was Evan and the look in his gaze as he'd stared at her, grazing her face with one finger that Sunday morning months ago.

It was all she had of him, that one moment in time. And it wasn't enough. She wanted more.

It wasn't fair. She would hurt him; but he was persistent. It was his own fault he hadn't heeded her warning that she was no good for him and left her completely alone. No, he had to go and call her house every single day and ruin everything.

Tears formed in the corners of her eyes and Ashley didn't bother to wipe them away. She rarely cried. Hadn't in months. Pent up frustration spilled out and dripped on her jean-clad knees. She wanted what everyone else did—a mate. Someone who would love her unconditionally for the rest of her days. Someone who would hold her in the night and not freak out when she woke up screaming, as she inevitably would.

She wanted Evan and to continue to deny that was ludicrous. Surely her infatuation with him was just that, lust. *Seriously, you've only spent a few hours with the man. You don't know him.*

Perhaps the best thing to do would be to see him again and prove to herself he wasn't the superhuman/supershifter creature she imagined him to be after months of blowing up his image in her mind until he was larger than life.

Yes, she'd been filled with lust for him every time she'd been in his presence, but it couldn't be real. Of course, Josh said it was. He'd told her when he met Samantha they'd known in an instant. She shivered to think about her brother in that light. He'd implied they'd barely made it out of Samantha's office and back to his place before…

Ugh.

And then Nathan had come along. Samantha had spent the entire next day with Nathan in an enclosed car. She said she'd managed to keep her hands to herself the entire drive to Alabama where they were headed to help Josh rescue Ashley.

Samantha had told her it was rough. Unimaginable. And that's how Ashley felt about Evan now. But was it real?

Only one way to find out.

~

"What are you doing here?" Evan stood at the front door, holding it open only enough to allow Josh to squeeze inside and hopefully leave the snow outside.

"Came to talk to you… Ashley asked me to."

Evan snapped his head up as he shut the door and turned to face Josh. "What?"

"Yeah." Josh smiled. "She asked me to invite you

over…if you want. No pressure. She wants to see you. She said, and I quote, 'tell him he doesn't have to if he doesn't want to.'"

Evan smiled. Then he narrowed his gaze. "You aren't just shitting me to arrange for us to be in the same room, are you?"

Josh shook his head. "Now why would I do that? You'd both stop speaking to me."

"So she actually called you and asked you to talk to me?" *Why don't I believe you?*

"Yes. I mean, first I went by my parents' house this morning to see her. I told her you were coming home. Guess I planted the idea. She called me about an hour ago." Josh grabbed Evan's coat from the rack next to the front door. He hadn't taken his own off or stepped farther inside. He held it up. "What are you waiting for?"

Evan grabbed the coat. He stuffed his arms into the holes in record speed. "If I find out you're bullshitting me, I'll have your ass, man."

"I know." Josh opened the front door for the second time and stepped outside. "See you later."

Evan jogged to his car. It was cold. No sense hanging around with the snow falling on his head. *Yeah, that's why you're running.*

He made it to Ashley's house in record time, in spite of the snow that continued to fall. He was lucky he'd been able to land this afternoon. Planes were still on time only because the temperature wasn't low enough to cause serious icing.

It was dark when he arrived at Ashley's and he

glanced at his watch as he approached the front door. Seven. He took a deep breath and lifted his fist to knock, but the door swung open before he could make contact.

"Evan." Paul Rice stood at the door ushering him in. "Josh said you might stop by."

Evan rubbed his hands together as he shut the door behind him. "Josh said?"

"Yes. He called a bit ago."

"Where is Ashley?" If Josh had duped him...

"She's downstairs. We turned the basement into a sort of studio. I assume she's painting." Paul motioned with a sweep of his hand for Evan to head across the room.

Laura stepped out of the kitchen as Evan reached the other side of the living room. "Evan. So good to see you. Go on downstairs." She opened the basement door and ushered him forward.

It felt like a giant conspiracy to fix him up. Except parents and brothers didn't usually work so hard to get their daughter and sister to unite with a mate.

God, she had better know I'm coming down, he thought as he made his way gingerly down the stairs.

When he reached the floor, he finally saw her. She stood behind an easel, her face lifted. A paintbrush dangled from several fingers. Red paint dripped off the end, and then she dropped the brush, and it fell to the floor.

She didn't seem to notice. Her gaze was locked on his and she smiled, her eyes twinkling.

"Hi," he murmured, suddenly feeling like a teenager

on his first date. He stuck his hands in his jeans pockets as he wandered toward her.

"Hi," she mimicked. "I guess Josh called you?"

Oh, thank God. He didn't have to kill anyone tonight. "Yes. He stopped by my house in fact. Said you wanted to see me."

She blushed, a deep shade of red that reached down her cheeks and her neck and across the exposed part of her chest that he could see in the V of her shirt. How far south did the blush reach?

She opened and closed her mouth a few times and then licked her lips. "I hope you didn't feel obligated. I mean—"

"Ashley," he cut her off, "nothing that concerns you will ever be an obligation. Never. No matter how much time you need, I'll still be here." He chuckled. "That's what teenagers call being whipped. Now I get it."

She smiled. "I wanted you to move on with your life. I'm not…good." She swallowed and he watched in fascination as her throat worked. "My mother said you call every day."

"I didn't want her to tell you that. I never wanted you to feel pressured. I still don't." He continued to inch toward her. "And you are too good. Don't be so hard on yourself. Nothing that has happened to you changes who you are inside." He'd arrived in front of her, and he set his hand on her chest, between her breasts. It was a bold move on his part. "In here." Her heart beat against his palm and he worked hard to keep from shaking.

"I… I thought if I saw you I could prove it was just infatuation."

"And?"

"It's not, is it?"

He shook his head. "It doesn't work that way. You know it deep inside. I do too."

"It won't lessen. I wanted it to go away. Even when you aren't in town, it's still there. Torturing me. Pleading with me from the inside out until I can't think or sleep or sit still."

He felt as his grin spread across his face. *Thank you, God.* He yanked his hand from her chest as though he'd burned it. He glanced at his palm to make sure it wasn't on fire. Irrational but real. And then he stroked a finger down her face and across her bottom lip. So full and pink and wet from her licking it.

Her tongue reached out to do so again, catching the tip of his finger.

He stifled a moan. "I'm sorry. Sorry for all you've been through and sorry this happened between us at the most inopportune time in your life. But please don't ask me to leave again. I need to be near you, in any capacity you can handle. One day at a time, one hour, one minute, one second. I'll do anything it takes to earn your trust and make you feel whole."

He released her lip and cheek and let his hand drop. He couldn't stand to continue touching her skin. It was difficult to think with the heat of her body melting his finger tip.

"Maybe I was wrong. Maybe it isn't as inopportune as it seems. Maybe," she lowered her voice until she barely muttered the last part, "Fate knows the right moment and I've been a fool to ignore Her."

"Perhaps." This was going so much better than he'd expected. "Did you ask me to come over so you could tell me all this?"

She shook her head. "No. I didn't have any idea what I was going to say to you. I actually thought if you came by I could prove to myself it wasn't real and we could move on."

He chuckled. "It's more real than ever, I believe."

"Yeah." She stepped back. "But I'm still going to need time. I'm hardly able to give my mother a hug yet. Or my father. Hell, even Josh can't touch me without making my skin crawl."

She paused and he watched as she caught her breath before she continued. "I'm going to fuck things up. I'm a mess."

He stepped closer, not allowing her the space she thought she wanted. "Never. There is no right or wrong. There is only what we make of it. I will earn your trust, Ashley. I promise. One second at a time."

Flashes of color caught Evan's eye in his peripheral vision and he turned to see the canvas on her easel. He gasped. "Oh my." The words slipped out unbidden.

Ashley turned toward the easel. "Yeah. I'm not sure what this is. I guess I had a weird day." She giggled. The sound made him stiffen. His cock jumped to attention at the tinkling noise coming from her sweet lips.

"That's one way to put it." He tried to ignore his dick and concentrate on her painting. Lots of colors bombarded him. He wouldn't say it was bad precisely. In fact, it made him feel. Not good though. It brought out a sense of confusion, the colors screaming at him in a cacophony of craziness. "Is this how you feel?"

"It's exactly how I feel." She didn't stammer.

He turned toward her once again. "Let me take some of that away."

She bit her lip and nodded. "I'd like that."

Evan reached for her arm and slid his hand down until he met her fingers. He grasped them lightly and gave a gentle tug, nodding behind him. "Let's sit." He stepped toward the couch.

"I'm all messy."

"You're perfect."

She pulled her hand free anyway and removed the paint-splattered apron she wore. After she dropped it on the stool behind her, she set her palm back in his, a sort of peace offering. The first advance she'd made on her own.

If he could hold her hand for the rest of his life, he'd be a happy man.

Ashley sat on one end of the couch, releasing his hand again. He hated the loss. She curled her legs under her in the corner and leaned against the arm to face him.

Evan sat as close to her as he dared. She smelled so good. Even the fumes from the paint didn't cloud her own scent. He'd remember it always, anywhere, anytime. "How are your classes going?"

"Good. Boring so far, but it's a start. I'm taking basic gen-ed classes to get my feet wet. It's going to take me a while to get my degree at this rate. I was hoping to build up to a full schedule."

"You have some college classes already, right?"

"Yes. I had thirty hours before…" Her voice trailed off and she ducked her head.

Evan sucked in a breath and held it. He berated himself inside for bringing it up.

"It's okay, you know," she muttered. "It's going to happen. There's no way to avoid four years of a person's life and pretend it didn't happen."

She was right, but that didn't make it okay on any level.

Evan reached for her hand again, instinctively. He needed to touch her. He grasped her palm and rubbed his thumb over the back. He flipped her hand over and grinned at the variety of colors sprinkled on her fingers. "Have you been painting a lot?"

"Yes. And most of them are a bit more defined than that one from today." She giggled again. God, he loved that sound.

"I want to see them sometime. You have such an artistic eye." He could get lost in her work. In fact he had a few of her pieces from before she'd been taken at his house. She didn't know it. Her mother had scrounged them up for him one day, and Josh brought them over. He hoped she could get back the mojo that existed before Damon the monster stepped in and ruined everything.

"Thanks. Most of them are scattered around my parents' house. I'll give you a tour someday."

"I'd like that." He squeezed her fingers, enough to emphasize his words.

"You suck the oxygen out of a room, you know," she blurted.

He chuckled. "That's not possible."

"Why?" She tipped her head to one side, scrutinizing him.

"Because there was no oxygen in the entire basement when I arrived."

"I'm a hot mess."

"Everyone is. You just have a few extra skeletons. But you aren't the only person with an ugly past who has gone on to live their life to the fullest. You deserve to be happy. I want to make that possible." He took a deep breath. "I'll do anything for you…including letting you go if you can't deal with having me around. But I'll never be far away. If you know nothing else about me, know that I'm committed to you for life. I won't take another mate. It's not meant to be that way."

"It happens sometimes. Josh told me. I've heard from others too."

"It does. That's true. But I don't know of anyone who flat out rejected their claiming on the grounds that they plain didn't feel worthy. Sometimes one party has deeper issues than we do. Drugs. Alcohol. Abuse." He paused, but then he went on. It was all true. "There are lots of reasons someone might decline a mate. What we have won't do it, at least not for me."

She sucked her bottom lip in between her teeth and he had to strain not to tug it out and keep her from making teeth marks or worse.

"You sent me away. I understood perfectly. I'm not

mad or resentful of your predicament. But over time I realized I'm also not ever leaving you. Not emotionally. I won't begrudge you your own feelings, but I also won't walk away. At least not entirely. You can demand I go. You can insist I not see you. And I will respect that. But I won't take another mate, Ashley. You're it for me." He lifted her palm to his cheek and smoothed her silky skin against his.

"That's a lot of pressure," she mumbled.

"It's how it is. I don't mean to sound harsh. I want you to know that no matter how long you need or what monsters you fight I will be here for you. I won't leave you. Ever. I can't."

"I understand."

"Do you?"

"Yes. I wouldn't have asked you to come tonight if I didn't feel at least some of what you're describing." She pulled her hand from his face and crossed her arms. "You can't crowd me."

"I know."

"I'm very leery about being touched."

"I know."

"I get claustrophobic when people are in my space." A tear ran down her face and she swiped it away with her forearm quickly without untangling her arms from under her breasts.

"It's okay."

"I hate that you're so kind."

He smiled. His heart swelled. He wanted to hold her. She couldn't do it. She was backing off, tucking herself away from him. He could understand that, and as much as it hurt, he had to remind himself it wasn't personal.

Her pheromones leaked from her skin. She wanted him as badly as her body could process the information.

"I will never intentionally hurt you...emotionally, I mean. I wouldn't dream of hurting you physically." He ached to hold her. God this was going to be hard.

"I can't have kids." She seemed to think she should lay all her cards on the table. Was she trying to entice him to run? Scare him off?

"I wouldn't care. But what makes you think that?"

She bit her lip again. "The fact that I don't have any."

Well, there's that. He hated to contemplate her having sex with that bastard. *Wait.* "Who says that's your fault?"

She looked away, embarrassment keeping her gaze above his head.

"He could have been wrong. Did you ever think it might have been him?"

"No." She was honest.

"Perhaps it was a threat to his masculinity that you didn't get pregnant and he made it up. Did you ever see a doctor?"

"Ha. Are you kidding? Not for four years."

"Well then. I rest my case."

"He said *he* did and that his quote—swimmers—were fine."

"I bet he did." Evan didn't want to discuss him anymore. He was a jackass and didn't deserve this much attention.

"Anyway, it doesn't matter since I can't imagine ever

having sex again." She jumped up from the couch and walked away toward the window. "This is a bad idea."

Evan took a deep breath and stood. He had a long road to haul, but he would succeed. "Slow down. No one's asking you to have sex. Stop worrying about the future. Let's live in the present for a while, okay?" He stepped up behind her and could see both their reflections in the wide picture window, so clearly it acted as a mirror. "Let me repeat. I will not pressure you. You will be safe with me. Always."

She crossed her arms again, a defense against the world. He set his hands tentatively on her shoulders and then let them settle when she didn't flinch. In fact, she calmed. She may not realize it yet, but whenever he touched her, her heart rate slowed.

"The pace I need is unreasonably foolish and you—"

He stopped her with a finger to her lips. "I'll decide what's foolish, and nothing about you fits the bill." God, he loved her. Loved? Yes, loved. He had no doubt. It just was.

Suddenly she turned in his embrace and leaned her head against his chest. She unfolded her arms and wrapped them around him, hugging him tight and shocking the shit out of him. "I don't deserve you," she muttered into his shirt.

"You do." His hands flailed behind her for a moment as he tried to decide what to do. Finally he settled on stroking her hair. He inhaled her scent and closed his eyes.

The way she pressed against him made it impossible

to hide his hard-on, and he would forever have a hard-on around her so it was unavoidable.

For long minutes she held on to him. She relaxed in small increments, her body settling against his in a perfect fit.

It wasn't enough, but it was heaven while it lasted.

CHAPTER 12

Ashley wasn't being fair. She knew that cognitively. She knew it as deeply and firmly as she knew he sported the hugest erection of his life and it was currently pressing into her stomach.

She didn't care. No—couldn't. She needed him and this was all she could muster right now.

She wanted to ask him to stay forever and let her torture him with her presence until he broke. But she wasn't that big of a bitch.

Was she in fact testing him to see if his words would match his deeds? How cruel.

She flinched and wanted to step away, to stop the madness. But she couldn't bring herself to let go and end the best moment of her life. Even though the moment had turned into several minutes.

She knew her breathing evened out and her chest stopped beating as hard as it had been. Calmness filtered into her. He did that to her. With a touch to her hand, she soaked in peace and tranquility. For the first time in years.

He wouldn't hurt her. Never. She knew that intellectually. If only she could tell her body that.

Not that she didn't react to him. She did indeed. Her pussy throbbed. It had since he'd stepped on the first stair on his way down toward her. She just didn't know what to do with the feelings he evoked. They scared her. They swarmed around the room and seeped into her skin. She felt both frightened and elated at the same time.

He set his chin on top of her head, so tentatively she nearly wept at his sensitivity. She squeezed his waist harder. It had been so long since she'd felt this safe and craved this kind of contact. Maybe it wouldn't be so bad after all.

She lifted her face and leaned back to see his expression.

His brows were furrowed, but in concentration, not anger. He was trying to read her.

"I'm all over the board with my emotions."

"It's okay." He stroked her hair and cupped the back of her head.

"Kiss me." She gasped, shocked at her forwardness and the fact she'd blurted those words out. She hadn't dreamed of going this far so fast—as if first base were a marathon.

He didn't move. In fact, his eyes narrowed. "Are you sure?" He stiffened.

So sweet. So kind. Too fucking sweet and kind, and he was killing her with his patience.

"Now. Before I change my mind. Now, so I know what it feels like to be kissed by someone who means well."

He hesitated, reading her, his gaze traveling all over her face. And then he leaned the few inches that separated their lips and grazed his over hers.

It wasn't enough. She needed more. Her body controlled this…thing. Not her mind.

She lifted up on tiptoes and deepened the contact. Her arms traveled up the hard length of his back and dug into his hair, pulling his head down toward her.

He tipped his face to one side and their mouths fit together like a puzzle, lips pressing into lips. And she moaned. Her first real kiss.

She'd been so innocent when Damon had snatched her. And he'd never kissed her. There had never been an inkling of passion behind his advances.

Her body came alive and she concentrated on Evan, letting Damon fall crushed beneath her feet. She ground her toe against the carpet for emphasis.

Of its own accord, her tongue reached out to graze the slit between Evan's lips.

Evan moaned and hauled her closer. She didn't flinch. She needed more.

He dipped his tongue inside her mouth and teased her with gentle swipes against the roof of her mouth, her cheeks, her teeth, her tongue. He tasted of…Evan…a flavor she would crave for the rest of her life.

She became aware of the rest of her body in a way she'd never experienced. Sure, she'd felt the hardening in the lower part of her belly in Evan's presence before, but now her entire stature was engaging. Her nipples stiffened. Her breasts felt heavy and she pressed them into his chest.

Her sex swelled inside her jeans and she squirmed against the pressure and need to rub her clit against the denim.

Evan broke the kiss. She couldn't see straight as he stepped back a pace and held her at arm's length. He took several long drags of oxygen before she could get her eyes to focus.

"Why...?"

"Oh, baby. You took off like a rocket."

"So?"

"So, one minute ago you told me you didn't think you would ever be able to stand being touched."

Oh, yeah that. I'm such a bitch. A tease.

"Don't look like that." He soothed a finger down the side of her cheek.

Her face was on fire. It burned against his cool finger.

He tapped her nose. "You're fucking gorgeous when you're aroused." He stepped back and let her go entirely. "Shit." He ran a hand through his hair and glanced around the room.

"I'm sorry." She felt his anxiety. She was cruel.

"Oh, baby. Don't be. This isn't your fault. Stop apologizing." He looked at her, but didn't reach for her again. "I just need a moment. I let myself get carried away."

"So did I," she muttered. Her face fell in shame. She was such a heel.

He stepped into her space once again and lifted her chin. "You're sexy and gorgeous and I will always cherish this moment. But, I don't want to rush things and risk you regretting our rate of incline later. Baby steps."

She didn't feel like taking baby steps right now, but he was right. If she didn't rein in her lust, she would risk regretting her decision to mate.

His finger felt cool against her chin, and when he stroked it up and down the length of her neck she gasped, a shiver racing from her head to her toes. "Please don't go," she pleaded. She wrapped her arms across her front again, hugging herself tight.

"Wouldn't dream of it."

"I meant...ever."

"Okay." *Except I have to work.* Damn. Hours ago he'd agreed to investigate Damon Parkfield and his drugs for The Head Council. He'd signed an agreement and a contract. Hell, he'd signed a non-disclosure clause that prevented him from mentioning the job to Ashley. He had no choice now but to work the case and lie to her about his job.

His shoulders slumped. "Except when I'm working."

"I thought you had expanded your company so you wouldn't have to travel so much? Josh said—"

"Yeah, that was before."

"Before what? Oh...me." She didn't hesitate between the two sets of words before she realized what he meant.

"It's not that so much. It's that I'm working on a case

that requires my attendance. I committed to the client that I would handle it myself. It's sensitive."

She narrowed her gaze at him. "Is it dangerous?"

He shook his head. "No. Don't worry about it, but I will have to travel until it's done."

"Oh." She couldn't prevent the deflated facial expression she knew she bore.

"Whenever I can, I'll be with you."

"I'm a pain in the ass."

"No you aren't. You're a woman with PTSD and I get that. You earned it. I'll chase it away. Slowly but surely. Trust me?"

She nodded. But she didn't feel good about what she was asking of him. She wanted to have her cake—hell, all the cake in the universe—and eat it too.

"It's late. You look exhausted," he said.

"I haven't slept well in…" *Four and a half years.*

∼

"I know. I'm here now. I won't leave. Tell me where you want me and I'll stay right there until you wake up." He glanced at his watch. Hell, it was late. Almost eleven. He'd been awake for hours. He'd been on a very early flight to Seattle and then another flight to St. Louis. Exhaustion would kick in. But would it win in a fight against the arousal he felt in Ashley's presence?

"Come on." She grabbed his hand and tugged him along behind her. He trailed her up the stairs and down a hall. It was quite. Her parents would have gone to bed by now. She stepped into a room on one side of the hall and shut the door with a quiet snick behind her.

She giggled again. "I feel like a teenager sneaking around behind my parents' backs."

"Yeah, well I don't think they will be opposed to my being here in this case."

"No, but it still feels weird." She pointed at a room off to the side. "The bathroom. Go ahead. I'll change."

He backed toward the door she indicated, not taking his eyes off her. She turned and he followed her with his gaze. Her ass fit so fine in her worn jeans. Her shirt hung untucked, the tail covering too much of her backside, but fluttering in a way that teased him about what lay beneath.

His back hit the wall and she spun around. "You missed the entrance." She pointed at the doorway and lifted an eyebrow.

"Yeah, yeah." Finally he turned and entered. He shut the door and gasped for breath. It wasn't as though he could jack off in the bathroom really quick while she changed. He was stuck with this hard-on for the night. And where did she propose he would sleep?

Oh, what did it matter? He wasn't going to sleep anyway.

He took his time, washing his face with her soap, brushing his teeth with his finger because it seemed wrong to use her toothbrush just yet and he didn't see another. After using the toilet, he returned, hoping he'd given her enough time to change while simultaneously hoping he hadn't.

She smiled and they danced around each other as

she entered the little bathroom and shut the door herself.

Evan stepped around her room, taking in her possessions. Most of her wall space was covered with paintings he recognized as her own. He knew which ones were pre-Damon and which ones were post. Her style had changed. It was darker now. Less innocent. And he silently cussed that motherfucker for the thousandth time.

The door opened behind him and he whipped around to find her padding across the floor.

What did she want him to do?

Her bed was full-sized. He could fit next to her, but barely. He wasn't a small man. Besides, the proximity would kill him. It was a bad idea. He twisted around, found a chair at her desk and whipped it to face the bed.

Ashley climbed under the covers and pulled them to her chin. "Don't," she whispered.

"What?" he asked as he sat facing her.

"Please. Lie with me. I know it's the most ridiculous request I've ever made, but I want you beside me." She patted the bed next to her and scooted her ass over until she nearly fell off the side onto the floor.

He stared at the arrangement for a moment and contemplated her request.

He couldn't do it and he found himself shaking his head.

"Please." Her eyes were huge when he glanced at her.

He wrung his hands together and pondered his fate. No man alive, wolf shifter or otherwise, could be expected to do what she was requesting. It was unheard of.

And yet Evan gingerly climbed onto the bed and lay alongside her as though it weren't the hardest thing he'd ever do in this life.

Hell, it probably wasn't. She'd be a bowl full of challenges before he claimed her.

And he knew he would. It was only a matter of time.

Ashley turned to her side, facing him. He didn't have to look to feel her gaze on his profile. He stared at the ceiling and willed his dick to settle down. *Not tonight, fellow.*

"This means a lot to me, Evan." She reached for his arm and squeezed his bicep with her tiny fingers.

He patted her hand against his arm and settled his fingers over hers. "Sleep, baby. I'll be right here."

She calmed. Her breathing leveled out in minutes. He knew when she was at rest and he smiled. It might be the death of him, but he'd made his little mate comfortable and taken away some of her pain and worry. It was worth everything.

CHAPTER 13

Ashley opened her eyes to find Evan lying on his side staring at her, his face inches from her own. A smile spread across his face and he reached to stroke a finger down her cheek.

"You're still here."

"Of course. You asked me to stay." He pulled back from her face and settled his hand along his side.

"I've never slept that well in my life. What time is it?" The room was filled with sunlight. It couldn't be very early.

"Almost eight. I'm so glad you slept well."

"Eight? As in nine hours of uninterrupted sleep?" She sat up and glanced around the room.

"Yep. And you barely moved." He reached for her hand and gently entwined their fingers.

"Did you sleep as well as me?"

"Not a chance. But I did get to study your profile for hours. You have the cutest little freckle right beneath your left eye." He grinned. "I have your face memorized. I will not lose you anywhere."

"That's…comforting," she said while shaking her head. "And wrong on so many levels."

He lay back then, releasing her hand, and stretched his arms over his head.

She hated the loss of contact. And she knew she was going to try this man's patience when it came to the speed of this mating. Or lack thereof.

She watched as his chest stretched out. His T-shirt rose with his arms, exposing his abs—the finest abs on any man ever. Thank God his gorgeous fit body didn't resemble Damon's scrawny ass. She would never mistake this man for her ex.

It was funny how she thought of him as her ex considering they'd never been officially married by human standards. A lot of shifters did marry in the human way in order to blend in with the world. Damon had never asked that of her.

Her gaze traveled down to the low jeans that rested at Evan's hips. The denim hugged him perfectly as though he'd worn the pair forever. She swallowed around the lump in her throat when she found herself staring at his package and jerked her gaze up toward his face. His perfectly chiseled jawline showed the faint sprinkling of hair from lack of shaving. He had closed his eyes and she stared at his lids, watching the way they danced around as his eyes moved beneath them. His mouth was shut, but in a loose peaceful expression. She had the urge to run her finger over his lips and memorize their texture.

And then she switched to craving the feel of those lips against her own again. He wouldn't have to compare to Damon in that department. She couldn't remember one instance when he'd touched her face, except with the back of his hand.

She leaned forward, learning his face while he rested his eyes. His breath mingled with her own, the faint mint from last night's toothpaste doing very little to cover his scent. A scent she would know always and forever. Even in a crowded stadium she would be able to identify him and hunt him down.

He licked his lips then and she moaned, startling herself and then flinching at her indiscretion. When she let her gaze flick to his eyes, she found him staring at her. How long had she ogled his lips?

He didn't move or give any hint to what he was thinking and somehow that gave her the strength to blurt out her next sentence. "Would you mind kissing me again?"

He stared at her and narrowed his gaze the tiniest bit, still as a statue. Nothing in his expression gave away his emotions.

Too many seconds went by and she felt a flush rise up her face. She jerked back and sat facing away from him, lowering her head toward her lap and wringing her fingers in front of her. *So stupid.* "I'm sorry. That was a dumb idea."

Evan slowly sat next to her. With calculated moves that gave her no reason to freak out, he grasped her shoulders and lay her back onto the mattress. He hovered over her, his brow furrowed more than a moment ago. Was he mad?

"Baby, you can have anything your heart desires at any time. You just shocked me, and it took me a second to pull my wits together. I want to be sure you make choices with your head and your heart every step of the way. I would kick myself if I thought I hurt you because you let the mating instinct overrule your good sense and sped toward the claiming at a pace you aren't ready to handle in your mind or in your heart."

He set a hand so lightly on her chest between her breasts. The blankets had fallen down to her waist and the only thing covering her was the T-shirt half of her pajamas. The warmth from his palm calmed her. Every time he touched her she calmed. The effect was the exact opposite of what she would have expected.

In her experience with human or shifter contact over the last several months since her rescue, she could barely tolerate the slightest grazing of skin—even from her own family.

But Evan... Evan could do no wrong. Instead of sending her heart into a racing dither, he slowed the pace with a touch.

She relaxed into the bed, calm, her thoughts not racing at all. She focused on only one thing—his lips.

"Ask me again."

She lifted her heavy eyes from his mouth, confused for a moment. And then it dawned on her. "Kiss me, Evan."

Without taking his gaze off hers, he lowered his

entire frame over her until his lips grazed hers in the slightest of kisses. Slow, steady, he consumed her with barely noticeable contact.

A millimeter at a time he let himself lower until all she knew was his perfect mouth in a sweet kiss that rivaled the one from last night. He nibbled her lips, not releasing her gaze.

And suddenly her calm became a storm. The perfect storm. Her comfortable relaxed body came alive and she wanted more. She wanted to know everything about this man who'd stolen her soul. She grabbed his biceps with both hands and pulled him closer. He resisted, but she managed to deepen the kiss. She let her eyes close against his piercing stare and tipped her head to one side so she could get a better angle on his mouth.

As though her tongue had a mind of its own, it reached out instinctively to lick the seam of Evan's lips. He startled, but only for a second. A normal person probably wouldn't have noticed, but Ashley wasn't normal. She was a shifter, and she was sensitive. Alert.

More alert than ever in her life.

His taste matched his scent, a deep male flavor that was all Evan with a hint of mint. When his tongue came out to tease her own, she heard a slight high-pitched moan that startled her.

Her eyes shot open as Evan pulled back. He was grinning from ear to ear.

She noticed several things at once. She was squeezing the life out of his arms. Her fingers ached. Her entire body was warmer than it should be. Evan looked pleased with himself. Her sex came to life beneath the blankets, demanding contact for the first time in years. And, perhaps most importantly, she wanted him to keep going.

"I want more." She licked her lips.

"I know you do, baby." He raised one arm and brushed her hair from her forehead with the tips of his fingers.

"Did I make that noise?"

"Yep." He smiled again and gazed into her eyes in that way he was developing a habit of doing. "And it was so sexy."

Her sex literally throbbed when he said sexy. She squeezed her legs together to hold back the ache. It didn't work.

"Kiss me again?"

"Not on your life." He chuckled. "I'm a good man, Ashley, but I do know my limitations."

She flushed deeper. *Did he just turn me down?* How mortifying. She closed her eyes and moaned for real this time. Embarrassment flooded her system. She released his arms and flopped her hands at her sides, wishing he would back away from her so she could endure her discomfiture alone.

"Don't freak out on me, baby." He soothed her forehead with his fingers, brushing them over both eyelids as he stroked her skin. "I can smell your arousal. It's intense and you know it as well as I do. It's perfectly normal. The call of mates rules the body. But you could easily get carried away. Like I said, I want your heart and your mind, not just your body. And I want those parts first."

Ugh. Why did nature have to arrange for her to mate the only sensible man born on earth?

He chuckled. "You do things to me I never thought possible."

I *do things to* him? *Jeez.*

She swallowed. Words wouldn't form. She concentrated on the V between her legs, unsure if she wanted the craving inside her to subside or grow. It was a conundrum.

"God, Ashley. You make me lose my mind." He sat up, his shadow leaving her space.

For a woman who couldn't stand anyone in her personal space or touching her, she sure felt bereft of his huge frame hovering over her.

He turned so he faced away from her and she opened her eyes a sliver to watch his back as he took deep breaths. She'd made him horny. If he was half as horny as her, he'd be hurting.

"I'm sorry," she whispered, setting a hand on his back. "That was inconsiderate of me. It won't happen again."

Evan jerked his gaze over his shoulder and frowned. "I hope it happens dozens of times, today in fact. I just wasn't prepared. You caught me off guard. I need to rein in the… little head." He cringed as he said it. "Sorry. I couldn't think of how else to put it. Didn't mean to be crass."

The little head. She doubted any part of this giant man was "little."

He sobered before he spoke again. "I'll be ready next time. Don't hold back on my account. Whatever you're ready for, I'm here for you. I'll live. I just knew you weren't ready for more than that kiss this morning. Am I mistaken?"

She shook her head. "That was my second kiss." *Now why did I have to go and admit that?* Her face flamed.

Evan's eyes widened. His mouth opened but no sound came out.

"With the exception of Paul Michaels. He kissed me on the playground in third grade. Said I was cute." She grinned, hoping to cover up her complete mortification over the admission. *What twenty-five-year-old woman hasn't been kissed?*

He found his voice. "I'm honored. I hope I did it justice."

"More than."

To her startled amazement, he reached for her, lifted her with both hands, and pulled her to sit across his lap.

To further her shock, she didn't mind a bit. She loved the way he took charge and handled her so gently.

"In that case, I shall kiss you again, this time a bit more thoroughly." He didn't lose her gaze as he spread one giant hand between her shoulder blades and steadied her on his lap. He took her mouth tenderly, but pressed into her, leaving nothing to the imagination.

Like a starving man, he consumed her, his tongue entering her mouth and tangling with her own in a duel that would have made her giggle if she weren't so consumed with need. Every cell in her body came alive. Her breasts swelled, seeming heavier than a moment ago. Her nipples puckered and brushed against the cotton of her T-shirt as though it were sandpaper.

And the things that happened between her legs weren't describable. Wetness, heat, tightness. She squirmed against his thighs, unable to dispel the consuming ache that built and built until she thought she would burst open from a simple kiss.

How the hell was the connection of their lips sending fireworks down to her sex?

Nothing. Absolutely nothing had prepared her for this moment. Everything they said about mating was true. Any doubt she may have held about the validity of Evan being her true mate fled the room. She'd never felt an inkling of this rampage of sensation flooding her body.

She squeezed her thighs together as Evan continued to devour her mouth. She wanted more. She reached into him deeper with her tongue, mimicking what her pussy demanded below. Her clit throbbed and she knew the tiny nub was no longer protected by its hood. It brushed against her panties as she squirmed.

Her palms grew damp with sweat where she grasped the material of her pajama bottoms. She couldn't move them. She had no idea where else to put them, and besides her brain cells were occupied commanding her pussy into action and sending her blood to her sex.

As Evan tilted his head the other direction to provide her with a new angle, she became increasingly aware of another factor. His erection was pressing into her thigh, huge and as obvious as a freight train.

Part of her screamed to reach out and touch it, learn

it, feel its strength. The rest of her concentrated on the enormous size of his shaft. She'd heard no two men were alike. She knew rationally that some were larger than others. But from the force of the bulge at her leg, she had to doubt the masculinity of her previous jackass of a partner.

She both longed to see his erection and feared the first time he entered her with it.

She felt like a teenage virgin dabbling precariously close to second base.

And considering the cold calculated way all her previous sexual experiences had been, most of them from behind, doggy style, she felt she almost owned that virginal status.

This time it was Evan who moaned. He released her mouth, leaving it swollen and puffy. She didn't have the energy to lick her lips. He set his forehead against hers and held her gaze. He seemed to constantly judge her through her eyes. And he was always dead on. He read her soul through the depths of her pupils with incredible accuracy, never missing his mark when he analyzed her feelings.

"I love you." His words startled her. "I know it's absurd and quick and we barely know each other, but I know how I feel, and I don't want to waste a moment of my life pretending anything other than that. Life is too short and filled with crazy twists and turns. If anything happened to either of us today, I'd want you to have known how I felt at this moment. I love you, Ashley." He kissed her lips again, a gentle peck to solidify his words.

She had no idea what to say.

And he didn't ask anything of her, not even with his eyes. He wasn't disappointed and didn't need reciprocation. In fact, he kissed her nose, her cheek, her ear. He nibbled a path around her face as though he'd won the lottery.

"I have to get home. I have an assignment. I'm in the middle of a job."

"What is it?"

He held her away from him and frowned. Finally he spoke again. "I won't always be able to tell you what I'm working on. It's usually confidential. And this project is no different. But I have a lot of papers to dig through and they will be arriving at my house at ten. It will take me a few days to organize the material before I have to hit the road again."

Deflated was the only way to describe how she felt. Her shoulders sagged against her will and all the air ran out of her lungs. He was leaving?

"Come with me? To my place."

She lifted her face, inhaling oxygen back into her lungs. He wasn't blowing her off after all.

"I'd really love to have you by my side, at least in my home, while I work. Would you mind?"

She found her throat, dry and cracking, as she tried to speak. "Of course." *Thank you, God.* If he had walked out the door at that moment and left her sitting on her bed, a complete hurricane of emotions, she might not have survived the day. "Let me take a quick shower and grab some things."

He set her on her feet and held her steady in front of him before releasing her. Reluctance was the emotion she read on his face, a slight dip that happened between his eyes every time he was unsure of something.

As she turned toward the bathroom, she let herself smile. She weighed less than she had yesterday, her chest lighter and floating above the ground, making her steps seem to hardly touch the floor.

CHAPTER 14

When the doorbell rang at ten o'clock sharp, Evan steadied his little mate with a touch to her leg. She lay on the couch curled into herself, reading a book, or pretending to. The sound of the doorbell had stiffened her entire frame and he ached deep inside at what Damon had taken from her. "It's FedEx," he whispered as he kissed her forehead. He patted her thigh and stepped past her.

The vision that met his gaze made him gasp as soon as he opened the door. He'd expected a package or maybe two, but not four gigantic boxes that bulged under the weight of too much information.

"Evan Harmon?" the man asked. He held out an electronic tablet. "Sign here." He hardly acknowledged Evan's nod of confirmation that he was indeed the man to whom the delivery belonged.

Evan signed and the young skinny driver jogged away, leaving Evan to drag the boxes inside himself.

It took a few minutes and it was fucking cold out. Drifts of snow blew inside as he worked.

"Jeez," Ashley said as she approached him, pulling her sweater around her waist. "You said you needed to do some research. I thought you meant you had a file to read. This will take you until July." She scanned the boxes.

Even though he had yet to officially claim his sweet mate, he could already feel her emotions. Her words were joking, mocking his lack of foresight concerning the amount of work he had to do, but her shoulders relaxed, her arms hung looser. She was relieved, hoping it meant he wouldn't leave her.

His chest hurt, an actual pain he felt all the way inside. Not only would he have to leave this woman he loved, but he would undoubtedly spend months chasing her ex around the country until he nailed the bastard to the ground, and all the while he would be forced to lie to her about what he was working on.

Shit. He'd signed an agreement. He'd stated emphatically he would not discuss this case with anyone. And he was certain that included Ashley. Besides, she would freak out if she knew what he was doing when he wasn't with her. Talk about stress.

Nope. He would have had to keep this project to himself even if he hadn't agreed to sign a non-disclosure clause with The Council.

"I admit it's more than I expected." He set his hands on his hips and took a deep breath before he proceeded to heave the first box over to the dining room table.

"Can I help?"

He grinned over his shoulder, the box balancing precariously in his arms. "You wouldn't be able to push one of these an inch, my love." He set the box down. He didn't want her near them anyway. He hoped he could set up shop at the table, be able to work in the dining room, keep an eye on her in the living room and kitchen and still avoid her eyes wandering in the direction of the files.

He plopped the first box in a corner and returned for another. "Sit." He pointed at the couch on the way by. "You're obscuring sensitive information," he teased. Maybe if he made light of his predicament, she wouldn't grow suspicious.

When he reached her, he physically turned her toward the living room and pointed at the couch. He hated her near the boxes, let alone between himself and the files. Even though he hadn't seen the contents yet, he considered them dirty. Disgusting. He wanted to vomit thinking about what he would learn inside them.

Ashley lowered herself onto the couch, but she sat straight and tall as she watched him drag each box across the room. He was a fit man, but it was a workout.

Before he opened the first box to get to work, he wandered back over to her side. Her scent had already permeated every crevice of his home. He loved it and cursed it at the same time. He had no idea how he was going to concentrate enough to actually work. "How about I set you up a room you can turn into a studio?" Was that presumptuous?

Hell, if he converted the spare room across from his ridiculous, secret, Damon-hunting hovel into a studio, they could actually see each other more or less across the hall and he could keep his project out of sight.

"I'd like that." She smiled and set her hand on his cheek.

He leaned into the touch, loving the feel of her skin against his. His worries surrounding this unconventional wooing were dashing from his mind. She might not be ready to rush to the finish line, but she wasn't unaffected by him either. He was sharp enough to know she needed him as much as he did her.

It was only a matter of time.

"I have to get to work. You good?"

"Yes." She lifted her book off her lap. It was for pleasure, but she had a few textbooks with her also. She intended to study at some point.

Evan stood and rubbed his hands on his hips. He took a deep breath as though fortifying himself for what lie in those boxes. All that did was fill him with more of her scent. He backed away as he exhaled and only managed to miss falling over the coffee table by an inch.

Klutz.

~

Ashley watched her mate bustle around opening boxes and pulling out files. She peered up at him over the top of the couch. She held a book in her hand, open, but she hadn't read a single word—not even before FedEx arrived. She wasn't sure the book was right-side up.

All that mattered in the room, the house, the planet was Evan and the way he moved around unpacking files. He was huge, especially compared to her. Broad and strong. How much time did he spend in the gym? His muscles bulged across his arms and chest as he heaved a box onto the dining room table.

"Did you play football?"

"Huh?" He lifted his gaze and stared at her quizzically, his head cocked to one side. And then a smile spread and he chuckled. "If I had a dollar for every time someone has asked me that." He resumed scrounging around in the box he'd set higher. "But, nope. God made me this way. I like to work out. Lift weights. Run. But I never played football, much to the dismay of the high school coach, who hounded me every year trying to recruit me for the team."

"Guess that's what tall people get about basketball."

"Yeah, no one ever asked me to play that sport for some reason." He winked at her and then heaved a stack of papers onto the glossy table top. "I have two left feet. I did nothing but trip over myself in gym class."

Ashley warmed inside. She loved this. This getting to know him. Watching him.

"How about you?"

"No. I never played football either," she teased.

"Really?" He lifted an eyebrow. "I'd have pegged you for a linebacker for sure."

"Yeah, guess the coach thought I was too scrawny. I never played a sport. I never left the art room. If my hands aren't covered with paint, my shirt isn't stained, and my hair isn't dripping with some acrylic substance, it wasn't a good day." She sat up straighter, letting her book fall closed in her lap.

"That's great, having a passion, I mean. Besides you, I'm not sure I know what my passion is yet." He paused, leaning on the box and staring her in the eye.

And just like that the temperature rose in the room. Heat crawled up Ashley's neck. She bit her lip and held his penetrating gaze. He wanted her and she couldn't help but love the feelings it evoked inside. The ball of lust that had formed in her stomach yesterday continued to grow.

Somebody wanted her. Not just anybody, but the sexy hunk of man currently suffocating her with his presence.

Ashley. Broken. Ruined. Fucked up beyond all recognition. And yet, Evan couldn't see any of that. All he saw was his mate. She read it in his eyes every time he looked at her. He wasn't putting on an act to be nice. He wasn't wooing her out of some grand sense of pity. No. He really wanted her. And the idea still boggled her mind.

Evan broke the connection. He shook his head as though he realized he'd been in a trance and turned back to his work, sitting on the nearest chair and opening a file. He tapped a pencil eraser on the table in rapid succession and then bolted up once more. "I have an idea." He held one finger up as though indicating she should hold on a sec, although she had no idea what she was waiting for.

Evan grabbed a black computer bag from next to the wall, yanked out the laptop and whipped it open on the table like it would self-destruct if he didn't hurry. He typed furiously for several minutes, pausing now and then to stare at the screen. Whatever the hell he was doing, it made her curious. But he was on a mission and she didn't interrupt.

Finally, he looked up with a triumphant grin. "There."

She lifted both brows. "Okaay."

"Don't you have some studying to do or something? You're making me...nervous staring at me." He nodded toward the computer he'd carried in for her and set next to the couch. "I assume your on-line classes require some sort of on-line work."

She glanced at her own computer bag and exhaled. "Fine. Okay, but you're acting peculiarly." She reached over the edge of the sofa and grabbed the case. No part of her had any desire to actually study, but she also knew if she didn't she would get behind in her classes.

"All in good time, baby." He turned back to his work and left her hanging on his words.

~

Two hours later, Evan jumped out of his skin when the doorbell rang. He'd finally gotten engrossed in his research and had completely forgotten he was expecting a delivery. Not that he'd lost track of every movement Ashley made. Nope. The woman distracted the hell out of him with her sighs and the tiny noises she made while she tapped away at her computer.

Her eyes were huge round balls of fear when he stood and headed toward the door. "No worries. I ordered a few supplies." He leaned over the edge of the couch and kissed her forehead on the way by. He found he would take any opportunity to touch her. The sweet torture of contact with her skin was always a conundrum. He ached for the contact, but then ached more from the contact.

He stroked one hand down her face as he stepped away to get the door, intensifying his lust. Making matters worse for his permanently stiff cock.

"Evan Harmon?" the man questioned as Evan opened the door.

"That's me." He reached for the electronic pad and scribbled his name for the second time this morning. A variety of boxes littered the front porch once again. This time, he knew well what the contents were. Nothing as ominous as research into the disappearance and drug trafficking of Damon Parkfield. Not this time.

As the man dashed back to his truck, Evan hauled several boxes inside. It took him two trips, but finally he shut the door and dead bolted it behind him.

"How many times a day do you get deliveries?" Ashley asked.

"Never. This is a first."

"You sure are popular."

"This time it's not for me." He smiled at her. "Come. Help me out."

She stood cautiously, her gaze roaming around the various boxes. As she stepped around the couch, she gasped. "What is all this?" She had to have recognized the writing on some of the packages.

"Art supplies."

"I can see that. Why?"

"It's your passion. You're bored without them."

"I was fine. You didn't have to do this." She rubbed her hands together in front of her, her body language defying her words. She was itching to rip open the boxes and examine the treasures they held.

"I wanted to." He heaved the largest oblong package up and headed toward the hall. "Come on. I have the perfect place for you to set up a studio." Evan nudged the first door on the right open with his foot and stepped inside. He set the easel down against the wall and rushed across the room to gather his belongings from the desk.

"Is this your office?" Ashley asked as she set another box down on his desk.

"It was." He stacked papers and files and gathered them up in his arms. "It's your studio now."

She shook her head, gasping. "You can't do that."

"Why not?" He glanced over his shoulder as he headed across the hall. He took a deep breath and turned the knob. This room had been designated as the Hunt-for-Damon office. He was seconds from transforming it into a real office.

"Because it's crazy. We barely started speaking to each other yesterday. You can't just ... move all your shit around and..." she voiced from her new studio.

Evan dropped his stack on the floor inside the Damon room. He glanced around, ensuring there was nothing particular that stood out and would give away any hint he'd been obsessed with finding Ashley's asshole ex. Somehow he didn't think she'd approve. And besides, now that he was working for The Council, he didn't have a choice. He needed to keep her out of this room and all would be good.

She was standing in the same spot when he returned. He wanted to touch her. Hell, he wanted to flatten her against the wall and engage in a lip lock. But he resisted. She was still fragile, and the best way to ease her stress was to keep the pace slow.

What he knew for sure was he wasn't alone, and that fact kept him moving. As he leaned under the desk to detach his desktop from the wall, he smiled. He wasn't close to being alone. Thank God for wolf senses and their hormones. It boosted his confidence scenting her. He both loved and loathed that she was so aroused.

Baby steps, Evan…

Hopefully when he got himself set up across the hall, he would be able to see her, but not have to inhale her essence with every breath. *Sure, you can tell yourself that, but you know good and well her scent has filled this entire house now and you are doomed to distraction.*

CHAPTER 15

By mid-afternoon, Ashley had a new studio she hadn't dreamed of owning in this house twenty-four hours ago. It had taken some rearranging, but Evan had moved all his belongings out of the room and tugged all her art supplies in. They'd worked separately for several hours, each organizing across the hall from one another.

Ashley had the better end of the stick it seemed. Evan had left the mahogany desk for her and a love seat sat against the wall under the window. She'd arranged her schoolwork and computer on the desk and filled the rest of the space with the numerous art supplies. The man had gone a bit overboard when he'd placed the order.

When she'd questioned him he'd simply shrugged. "I didn't know what you might need," he'd said.

"You could've asked."

"And ruin the surprise?" He'd winked and moved on.

As she sat at the stool in front of her easel, she

watched Evan across the hall. He had placed his desktop computer on a folding table. The rest of the room was filled with two other long folding tables that were covered with a haphazard spread of papers. Whatever he'd been hired to do, the case sure had a lot of baggage.

Midway through the rearrangement they'd stopped for lunch. Evan had made sandwiches and they'd sat at the kitchen table as if they did so every day.

What she wanted to do was drop everything and pad across the hall. She closed her eyes, visualizing leaning over him while he worked, her hands running across his shoulders and down his chest until her mouth could nibble on his ear.

Her vision was ridiculous. First of all, she'd never wanted any such contact with another person, at least not since she'd been an adult. And second of all, Evan hadn't said so in specific words, but she got the distinct impression she wasn't welcome to peer at his massive research.

It was some top-secret project. He'd only said the client who'd hired him for this was loaded and wanted results.

She knew he was going to take several days to read through the boring throng of pages, but then he was going to have to leave town again.

It was the nature of his job. Private Investigators did occasionally have to investigate.

Considering the ramifications of him leaving town made her heart beat faster. She tried to ignore the reality, but it loomed in the back of her mind.

Meanwhile, she had other issues to consider. She

was playing house with the man of her dreams and she couldn't—or wouldn't—let him claim her. How long could she keep this up without irritating him? Eventually he was going to crack. If he was as aroused as she was, and she knew he was, he would only be able to take so much of her hesitation before it started to leak out in his demeanor.

She rubbed her hands on her jeans. She couldn't work. The room was all put together—everything in its place. Her laptop sat open on the desk. She could work on her school assignments. She could paint. She could read one of the books she'd brought.

But instead all she managed was to stare at Evan's ducked head, wishing she had the guts to go to him. She wanted to feel the strength of his muscles under her fingertips. Every time she touched him, she calmed. Well, her inner turmoil soothed. She couldn't say the same for her sex drive. It did not calm.

She stared, unable to stop herself, not wanting to do anything else but watch the top of his head, the way his hands moved around, rearranging papers, opening folders, scribbling notes.

"You're going to bore a hole in me," he said without looking up.

Ashley flinched, embarrassed, but then she realized he was teasing her. She glanced at the canvas on her new easel, but had no inclination to dip her brush in the paints.

When she looked back, Evan was stalking toward her, a smirk on his face.

Normally she would have been horrified by such a

look, but in the last day she'd grown close enough to him to realize he would never harm her. Instinctively she knew this. If Damon had looked at her that way it would have been followed by a backhand to the face.

Evan's hands didn't twitch at his sides to go with his expression.

When he reached her, he circled behind her and picked up the brush she'd set next to the pallet. He dipped it in orange paint. She couldn't imagine what he was going to do next, nor was she prepared for what happened.

While she stared at the canvas assuming he was about to attempt to create art, he tapped the brush to her nose.

Ashley gasped. She swiveled on her stool to face him. "Why'd you do that?" she asked, a giggle bubbling up from her chest. She swiped at the sticky spot on her nose, undoubtedly smearing it, and spread orange all over Evan's face, shocking herself.

She sucked in a deep breath when she looked at his expression. He narrowed his gaze, but then casually tapped the brush into the blue acrylic next.

Frozen in stunned shock, she couldn't bring herself to duck as he painted her forehead. And then his face broke and he laughed. He set his own forehead against hers, rolling it from side to side until his skin was smeared with the blue paint and they were a matched set. "You're too serious."

"Me? You're the one buried in work over there. I'm sitting here minding my own business." She pointed at the stool beneath her.

"I don't see any evidence you've minded any business whatsoever." He spread his arm in an arc to indicate the pristine condition of the room that had this morning been his office. "All I've seen you do is study my profile." He lifted both eyebrows, teasing her again. And then he dipped all five of his fingers in her paint, coating each one with a different color.

He wiggled them in the air, stretching his arm toward her clean canvas.

She gasped and grabbed his forearm. "Don't you dare. Those are expensive."

"I know. I bought them." He stretched farther, almost reaching the white surface.

She jumped up from the stool and put herself between him and the easel, shoving at his arm. "I'm not kidding." Her effort to thwart him backfired when she bumped into his hand, causing his fingers to drag across her shoulder and down her arm.

Or maybe he did it on purpose. In any case, a rainbow of colors now streaked down her T-shirt. She grabbed his wrist, but he was stronger than her and he twisted out of her grasp easily to dip his fingers back in the paint. "I think I like this canvas better anyway." He stroked the acrylic right down the center of her face.

It had been years since Ashley had engaged in anything so...silly. She jumped out of his reach, backing up across the room. But he was relentless and determined to annoy her. After dipping his hand again in the colors, he darted forward. She leaped to the side, feinting right but going left. He missed her face that time, but his hand landed in her hair, tangling in the length.

"Oops," he lied. "Look what I did to your hair." He picked up the long locks and grinned.

Ashley took another step back, trying to dislodge Evan, but she hit the wall.

He crowded her, his hand, still wrapped in her hair, landing on the wall next to her face. "You look so fucking sexy when you aren't trying to maintain the serious façade," he whispered. His voice came out shaking, deep, gravelly.

Ashley licked her lips, her shock over his behavior turning to lust at the look in his eyes. She squeezed her legs together and smashed herself into the wall. She should feel claustrophobic. In fact, she hadn't been cornered like this by anyone well-meaning for years. But all she could think about was his lips.

Her gaze landed on the full bottom one, eyeing the orange paint smeared into the corner. "Kiss me," she blurted.

Evan lifted his free hand to her cheek and cupped her face. "May I?"

"Please."

He lowered his face slowly, his eyes never leaving hers. He'd kissed her last night and then again this morning, but this was different. This time she knew with certainty she was his.

Evan tugged on her chin, his thumb pressing down until she opened her mouth. When his lips stroked hers with the barest pressure, a shiver swept through her body. She reached with both hands to grasp his forearms and steady herself.

Instead of intensifying the kiss, Evan reached out with his tongue and licked a circle around her lips. So intimate, the touch made her vision blur, and her eyes fluttered shut. She concentrated on nothing but his mouth, his breath mingling with her own, each inhalation sharper than the last.

She squeezed his arms tighter, undoubtedly leaving marks from her fingernails.

His tongue grazed her top teeth, and he flinched from the sensitivity behind her lip. Each stroke tickled the inside of her mouth and goose bumps rose all over her arms as he teased.

And then in an instant, he consumed her, a moan escaping his lips as he tipped his head to one side and pressed his mouth into hers. The pressure was welcome. She needed more of him. Anything would be better than the teasing flicks of his tongue against her lips.

She let him duel with her tongue, learning the feel of his mouth, his taste. She'd never been kissed like this. Even last night paled in comparison. Her entire body reacted to his mouth and she arched her torso against his, trying to increase the contact with him.

He got the message and stepped closer, straddling her legs and pressing his body into hers.

His cock nestled against her belly and she quivered at the firm length of him against her. Part of her was dying to know what he looked like, how he felt. And that section of her brain was taking over, slowly seducing her in rhythm with Evan's lips.

She pulled him closer, her breasts aching for any sort of contact. They felt full and the tips poked against her bra, rubbing the cotton material, pleading for more. Even the pressure of his chest against her own was better than nothing.

Still Evan kissed her. He made love to her mouth so intimately she lost all ability to think. He was a trained master, tipping his head left and right, angling her face with both hands now to suit his needs. A low hum continuously escaped his lips as he seduced her.

And God, she never wanted him to stop. No matter what the consequences, she needed this more than her next breath.

She jumped when his toes hit the wall with two soft thuds. Truly pinned, she knew deep in her mind she should be frightened, but it didn't come. The fear never reached the surface. Nothing about the way Evan touched her made her concerned for her safety, neither physically nor emotionally.

Warmth suffused her body; a tingling entered her limbs. Her temperature seemed to rise with each breath either of them took, bringing their chests in closer contact. Ashley released her grip on Evan's forearms and wrapped her arms around his body, pulling him against her.

He resisted. The stiffness of his rigid stance was evident.

Finally, he released her lips. He set his forehead against hers and peered into her eyes as she widened them. The loss of his mouth was unacceptable. Why did he stop?

She searched his gaze for anything that would answer her question.

His mouth tipped up on one side in a grin. "You liked that."

She could only blink. She more than liked it. She wanted more.

He held her head with both hands, caressing her cheeks with his thumbs. His smile dropped as he lowered his lids and inhaled deeply. "You're so aroused. You're going to kill me."

Those words made her tighten her pussy. Moisture leaked out to dampen her panties. Her jeans felt too tight, the seam pressing into her clit and threatening to buckle her knees.

And she wanted more. "Don't stop," she murmured.

"Baby…" He circled her mouth with one finger.

Her swollen lips opened in attempt to capture his finger.

"Any more of that and I won't be able to stop myself." He heaved for oxygen as he spoke.

"I don't want you to stop." Had she said that? Her body trembled, but it was true. She was done dancing around the elephant.

He stared deep into her eyes, seeming to read her soul, making her feel exposed from the inside out. Long deep inhales filled his lungs.

She barely breathed herself. She couldn't and remain standing. While he scented her she had to keep herself in check or she really would collapse against the wall.

His masculinity oozed from every pore, calling to her on a primitive level. It wasn't to be denied and she couldn't fight it any longer. But still she couldn't inhale too much at once or she feared she would faint.

"Are you sure?" he asked. He tapped her temple with one finger. "Here, I mean? I know your body is primed for mating, but I need to know your mind is on board also. I won't do anything to jeopardize your mental progress. I would never be able to forgive myself if I did anything that upset you."

"I'm more sure than ever in my life. Claim me, Evan. Erase all the bad experiences in my past and smother them into nonexistence with new ones…true ones." She was sure. Suddenly nothing else mattered except being with Evan, closing the gap between them and letting him into her heart, her mind, her body.

Evan smoothed his thumb over her forehead, her cheek, her chin. "You have paint everywhere." He smiled.

"So do you." She imagined she looked just like him.

"I want to paint the rest of you one of these days."

She lifted her brows. Paint me? She knew from the context he meant that literally. Not that he wanted to paint a picture of her. No. He wanted to paint *her*. Her fingers shook pondering the idea, and she gripped his shirt where she held him.

He wove his hands through her hair and tugged. "There's paint in your hair too."

She didn't care. *Why is he so worried about the paint all of the sudden?*

He played with the locks for several moments before

he let his gaze wander back to hers. "I'm trying to slow down." He grinned. "It isn't working."

"Well, stop. I don't want you to." She bucked toward him, reminding him with her body how firm he was against her belly. She wished she had the balls to release his back, drag her hands to his front, and circle his cock. But she wasn't that bold yet.

"You'll stop me at any time...if you feel uncomfortable?"

"No."

He froze.

She lifted her gaze to his once more and smiled. "I want you to claim me. Please. I'm burning up inside." She squirmed against him, the most brazen thing she could do. Even that act brought a flush to her cheeks she could feel deep inside. She released the fistful of T-shirt she held and flattened her palms on his back, grazing toward his ass.

Evan pushed off from the wall, breaking contact. He took her hand in his and pulled her behind him as he stepped into the hall and then entered the next door on the right.

His bedroom. She hadn't been in this room yet. He'd given her only a brief tour of the house, but when he came to that room, he'd only pointed and declared it to be the master bedroom. She'd assumed he hadn't wanted to make her uncomfortable. At the time she'd been relieved. Now she wanted nothing more than to explore his inner sanctuary.

She wanted to know everything about him.

He released her in the center of the room and

sauntered toward a door to the left. Running water told her it was the attached bath.

She spun slowly and soaked in…Evan. Dark colors filled the space. Gray, black, navy. Even his comforter was a deep navy. His bed was unmade. The sheets were the same deep blue to match the bedspread.

She inhaled long and slow. The house was naturally filled with his scent, but this room was more potent. She didn't notice he'd returned to her side until he held a cloth up and began to wipe the paint from her face. He took such care, his precision and concentration bringing a lump to her throat.

If she'd been a different woman in a different time with a different history, she'd have grabbed the cloth, tossed it to the ground, and slammed him against the wall to keep him from stalling.

But she was who she was, a grown woman not remotely ready for anything quite so bold. Instead she held her breath and watched his eyes flicker over her face. The smeared colors on his own forehead and cheeks were gone, just the faint edge of colors left at his hairline.

Finally he dropped the wash cloth and cupped her face once more, taking her lips in a kiss that rivalled the last. Firmer. More demanding. He entered her with his tongue as soon as their lips collided.

She fell into the kiss, concentrating on the feelings it evoked. A tight wire ran from the connection of their mouths to her sex. Her clit jumped to attention, something she'd never experienced in the past.

She didn't realize they'd shuffled across the floor until her legs hit the side of the bed.

Evan's hands wandered down her frame, his palms spread against her back. His hands were huge splayed open like that. He seemed to encompass her entire back and still his thumbs stroked very close to the edges of her breasts.

God. She wanted those hands on her. She broke the kiss, sucking air into her lungs.

"You okay, baby?"

"Too okay." She shook her head, trying to gain a small piece of control. She couldn't think of anything except the need building between her legs.

Evan tapped her feet apart with one of his and pressed his thigh between her legs.

She sucked in a deep breath when his warmth snuggled against her pussy. And then she moaned. Her hands trembled where she held his shirt once more. "Evan?"

"You're so aroused, baby." He rubbed her back lower. "Your body is so ripe for my touch." His hands landed on her ass and he squeezed.

A squeak escaped her lips and she ground herself against him harder, needing the pressure. Feelings she'd never experienced came to the surface. "I've never..."

"I know. Just let go. Feel. It's going to be so good." He reached between her legs from behind as he spoke and stroked his fingers across her sex.

She nearly jumped. "Oh God." Her vision blurred. She tipped her head back, seemingly unable to hold it upright any longer. All she knew was the feel of his fingers stroking through her slit and she wanted the jeans gone.

So this is what mating feels like...

Evan's fingers left her crotch and he pushed her shirt up with both hands until he met her armpits. "I'm going to undress you, okay?"

God. *Okay? Fuck no. Not just okay. I insist.*

He must have read something in her face because he gave a slow grin and then pulled her T-shirt over her head.

Welcome cool air hit her heated skin as he leaned away from her to soak her in with his eyes. "So gorgeous." He smoothed his fingers over her bare skin, starting at her belly and working his way upward. He skipped her chest, still covered by her sensible bra, and traced a line along the top swell of her aching breasts. The bra seemed two sizes too small and her nipples flattened tight against the cups.

Evan reached behind and expertly popped her loose.

She sucked in a breath and bit her lower lip as he revealed her to his gaze. The release of pressure forced her to exhale slowly between her teeth, leaving her breasts heavy.

Reverently, Evan circled her waist with both hands. His gaze never left her nipples as he watched her chest rise and fall.

She watched his face. Would he find her attractive? Intellectually she knew she was not the ugly creature her ex had insisted she was. Therapy had straightened out her body image drastically in the last months.

However, nothing could stop her from worrying about his reaction.

Gentle fingers caressed her globes as they seemed to grow under his touch. "So fucking sexy, Ashley." He circled her nipples simultaneously, making her arch into his touch.

She released her bottom lip, feeling the sting where her teeth had gripped.

She couldn't help but watch her nipples pucker and she silently pleaded with Evan to touch them directly.

Instead he weighed both breasts in his hands while she held her breath.

Suddenly he didn't just touch the tips, he pinched them, and at the same time he lifted his thigh to press into her pussy.

Ashley screamed. She still had her jeans on and she squealed like a woman in the throes of sex. An elusive something pulsed in her sex, demanding exit.

She flushed with embarrassment when she was able to see into Evan's dark brown eyes once more. Her face and chest heated to a new high.

His deep gaze darkened as he stared at her. "I've got you," he mumbled. "So fucking responsive…" He continued to toy with her nipples, pinching and releasing, soothing and repeating.

When she didn't think she could breathe anymore, he lowered his fingers to her jeans and released the button. "Look at me."

She let her hazy gaze settle on his again.

"You okay?"

She nodded.

"I want to see all of you. May I?"

She nodded again and bit her bottom lip between her teeth once more.

Not releasing her gaze, Evan lowered her zipper painstakingly slowly. He let the pressure of his thigh ease until he removed it.

Ashley held her breath. She was more aroused now than while he'd been pressed against her. She needed more, not less. Her body had its own agenda and demanded release.

Her legs shook as Evan kneeled in front of her. He pulled off her shoes and socks, lowered her jeans with her panties, and then tugged them off first one leg and then the other.

Naked now, she had a surge of self-consciousness. Her gaze shot in every direction. "You're still dressed." She crossed her arms and drew her legs together.

Evan pulled his shirt over his head and dropped it to the ground. "Better?"

She couldn't respond. His chest was a giant expanse of muscle and tanned skin. She had the urge to lick across his nipples. So hard, his pecs flexed as she watched.

Evan lifted her around the waist and set her down several feet back on the bed. "Just relax. Nothing is going to happen that you don't beg for." He climbed up at her feet where her legs were bent, her knees together, her heels digging into the mattress.

Beg?

She would never beg. What did he mean?

She narrowed her gaze and he chuckled. "You will." Had he read her mind?

"Lie back." Evan gently eased her onto his cool sheets. Her head landed on his pillow, the soft fall incongruent with the tight ball in her belly.

She stared at his chest and then let her gaze lower to his jeans. His cock bulged so full; the button on his jeans threatened to pop. She wanted to see him completely naked as he was seeing her, but she also feared the size of him behind that denim. If she wasn't mistaken, he would be far larger than the only man who had ever taken her.

Evan started his soothing strokes again, his fingers dancing across her skin, down her arms, across her belly, around her breasts. So erogenous. She'd never known. Damon hadn't paid any attention to her chest except to complain about how small she was.

Evan brought her back to the present when he tapped her nipples. "So pink. I love how they respond to my touch."

She moaned. Wetness leaked between her rigid legs. She gripped the sheets on both sides with her fists. She didn't know quite what she wanted him to do, but she was wound up like a top, her body threatening to spin out of control and leave her with vertigo.

Evan dragged his fingers down her body until he reached her thighs. "Open for me, Ash. Let me see you."

Her legs quivered. The idea of him staring at her pussy with the same intensity as he had the rest of her was daunting. Too much. She glanced at the window. The curtains weren't open far so the room wasn't bright, but they weren't closed all the way either. A few inches allowed plenty of light into the room. He wouldn't miss an inch of her with his piercing gaze.

He didn't say anything else. Instead he seemed to sense her hesitation. She didn't have her legs squeezed together. They were open a few inches, but her bent knees were rigid to the point of aching.

Evan knew how to play her though. He was the master of her body. He grazed his fingers up and down her thighs, first the top and then underneath, and then he teased the skin between them until she gasped and her knees fell open on their own.

"That's it, baby. Relax."

He kept saying that, but she was unable to comply. Her stomach tightened into a ball.

Evan pressed her thighs wider and upward, forcing her knees to bend more as she exposed her most private parts to his gaze. Before touching anything directly, he pulled her lower lips apart and breathed in deeply until his eyes fluttered. "God, Ashley. You are so aroused." He glanced back down at her pussy. "So wet. Are you always this wet?"

She didn't move. She gripped the sheets with her fists and pleaded with her mind for him to fucking claim her already.

He stroked one finger through her folds and she shot off the mattress, gasping, her heels digging into the bed to lift her torso.

She tried to swallow as she lowered herself back down, but her mouth was too dry. *OhmyGod*.

"Oh, baby. You are the sexiest creature alive." He did

it again and her belly hollowed, but she didn't lift as high this time.

She watched as he adjusted his cock with one hand. "I'm going to come in my jeans." He let his gaze settle over hers. The deep brown of his eyes was almost black now.

When he stroked through her folds a third time, he chuckled. "So squirmy." He settled his other hand on her belly above her clit and pulled the skin back.

She could feel the moment air wafted across the nub and she flinched.

Evan gathered her moisture with two fingers and swirled them up to circle her exposed clit. "Like a little pearl..." He kept circling, not touching her where she needed it most. "What do you need, Ash?"

Her eyes widened. Was he kidding? No way could she talk right then.

"I could stroke it, pinch it, lick it..."

Oh, yes. One of those things. Hell, all of them.

He smiled, his gaze jerking between her clit and her eyes. "I can't decide. I want to watch your clit as it responds to my touch, but I want to see the green of your eyes deepen to a deep ocean color also."

He swirled, circled, played with the surface of her pussy until she trembled with need. "Please," she finally pleaded.

"Please what, Ash?"

"Please claim me, already, Evan." The words were chopped, deep, glottal. She didn't recognize her voice.

"No way. Not yet."

Was he serious? She'd never wanted anything so bad

in her life. She couldn't imagine how or why she'd gone this long putting off this inevitable experience. The entrance to her pussy pulsed with the craving to be filled. She squeezed against nothing, grasping only at the walls of her channel.

He would need lube. She twisted her head from side to side, straining to see if he had some ready. She hated to ask. Surely he knew. Damon had always said his cock ached inside her dry cunt because she was so frigid.

She froze and glanced back down at the spread of her legs. She was wet… Very wet. She didn't remember ever being this wet. Clearly not frigid. No. That had been her body's response only to Damon. Perhaps Evan wouldn't need anything at all to ease into her. She hoped he would go slow. Suddenly she feared the moment he entered her for the first time, stretching her wide and scraping against her insides.

She had to ask. It would ease her fears if he used a lubricant. It would ease the possible burning inside her. She blurted out the words. "I think you'll need to take your pants off and do you have any lube?"

He stopped and looked at her face, his fingers poised at her entrance. "I'm not ready to take my pants off and why the hell would I need lube? You're so wet, I'll have trouble staying inside you."

She pinched her lips together and closed her eyes. Maybe he was right. And then he slid a finger deep inside her. She moaned loud.

He curled that finger and brushed it over the top of her channel as he pulled out. The next time he pressed in, *he* moaned. "God, Ash. You are so wet. What did that bastard do to you?"

She didn't answer. She doubted he really wanted to hear it anyway.

He added a second finger to the first and entered her as far as his hand would allow, scissoring inside her until she felt the pressure building to a crescendo. His palm planted firmly against her pussy, bumping so close to her clit but not quite touching the very nub that demanded attention.

"I want you to come, Ash." He finally stroked her clit with the fingers of his other hand as he spoke. "I want to see you come apart at my touch. Will you give that to me?"

She gritted her teeth. She'd never had an orgasm. Didn't even know how. Would he be disappointed? "I can't."

"Oh, baby, you can. Lots of times." He pulled his hand out and added a third finger. So tight. He stretched her.

She bucked into his touch. The ache she felt inside, the ball of nerves that threatened to explode, that was what he meant.

He flicked a finger over her clit in rapid succession.

She dug her heels harder into the bed. *Oh God.*

Her head rolled back and forth as she concentrated on his touch. Her brain turned to mush, unable to think about anything but his fingers tormenting her body. Suddenly he pushed deeper and pinched her clit with his other hand at the same time.

She screamed. Her entire body seemed involved in

the noise. Her clit throbbed as it pulsed. She fell off the edge of a cliff into a deep gorge below, falling, falling, falling, until finally she floated gently back and forth toward the ground. The orgasm consumed her, swallowing her whole. Even the tactile sense of the sheets beneath her disappeared as she centered all her attention on the fingers stroking inside her and the pinching pressure on her clit.

He slowed as she settled back to earth, easing his pressure until he released her inside and out. He continued to soothe her lower lips with his touch as she flinched, still not completely separated from the orgasm.

CHAPTER 16

Evan watched his mate's face as she floated back to earth. The moment her eyes connected with his and realization dawned on her, she blushed a deep red. "Oh..." She glanced around. "You... I..." He watched her throat as she swallowed embarrassment.

"You were so beautiful. Have you never had an orgasm before?" He wanted to suck those words back the moment they left his lips. She hadn't. That was clear.

She tried to draw her knees together, but he stayed between her legs. The last thing he wanted was for her to shut herself off from him. "I'm sorry." He soothed her thighs with both hands, trying to relax her stiff legs. "Thank you. That was a gift I will never forget."

"I don't know what you did with your magic fingers, but..." She smiled, a coy grin that included tipping her head to one side. Her embarrassment fled; or she chased it off. "I don't think whatever that was will consummate the claiming."

Evan released a breath he hadn't known he held. He

still knelt between her legs, but he released her to pop the button on his jeans and wiggle out of them, taking his underwear with them. It was probably awkward. He felt like a gangly teenager eager to have sex for the first time. He somehow managed to discreetly reach into the pocket and pull out a condom, which he set on the bed next to him without her noticing.

She didn't say a word. Instead she watched him, her eyes growing wider as he revealed his cock to her gaze.

This time her knees snapped shut. His dick bobbed in front of him, stiffer than he could ever remember. Pre-come leaked from the tip as though pleading with him to get on with the show.

Evan wrapped his hand around his length and moaned as he stroked himself from the base to the tip.

Ashley used her heels to scoot back a few inches. Her eyes bugged out. "That's not… You can't…"

Her sentences were chopped short and she licked her lips afterward, perhaps not realizing she had said nothing coherent. He knew what she was thinking. That bastard Damon must have had a tiny dick. Either that or he never let Ashley see it while he raped her.

A chill went down his spine and he shook thoughts of her ex from his mind. He would erase all memory of the jackass soon enough. He only hated that Ashley had gone through all that in the first place.

He settled his gaze on her eyes again, watching her as she stared at his cock. The darn thing grew as she watched, eager, willing, hell, demanding.

He wouldn't pressure her. If she called a halt right

now, he would stop. It would be difficult, but he would do it.

He waited.

She took in his length. Moments past while he watched her chest rise and fall, slowing with each breath. Finally her legs fell open.

She reached for him with one hand, grabbed his arm, and pulled him toward her.

Evan settled over her body, lowering himself in the V of her legs until his cock rested at her entrance and his chest brushed against hers. And then he kissed her, a sweet gentle kiss, slow and precise while he waited for her to part her lips for him.

Ashley tipped her head to one side, grasped his biceps with both hands and angled for a deeper kiss. She licked the seam of his mouth brazenly, coming out like a tortoise from her shell. When she pulled her mouth away and turned her head to one side, he feared she was panicking.

She heaved several breaths, not making eye contact. Her fingers squeezed the muscles on his arms. "God… Evan." She turned to face him, inches separating them. "I need you. I never thought I could feel like this. I had no idea… Please… Claim me."

A smile spread across Evan's face. He felt the furrow of his brow as it relaxed. This was really going to happen. He pushed up to his knees with both hands, grabbed the condom from the mattress, and ripped through the foil pack. As he rolled the rubber onto his cock, he watched her face.

"I'm telling you, you don't need that." She rolled her eyes as if he were dense.

Evan smiled. "And I'm telling you I do. I can smell it on you. Not only can you get pregnant, but you're ovulating this week. So, humor me…unless you want to start a family in nine months."

She gasped. "You can smell that?"

He nodded. "And believe me, I don't care if you do get pregnant. This mating is forever. Whatever happens, we'll deal with it. But, I think you need more time to find yourself before we add a baby to the mix."

She shook her head. "I'm not sure I believe you, but whatever." She grasped his forearm and tugged him on top of her again. "Please. Stop chatting. I'm burning." Her eyes were glazed once more.

His chest swelled. He affected her. He alone brought that look to her face. And he alone would treasure this gift for all time.

She bucked her torso into him.

His cock nestled at her entrance. "Look at me." He waited while her vision cleared and he knew she was seeing him. "Keep your eyes on mine." Evan wanted to be sure she never doubted who she was with while he claimed her.

She sucked in a breath and held it when he nudged her entrance with his cock.

He paused. "You okay?" He rested both elbows alongside her head. With one thumb he stroked her hairline. "Say the word and I'll stop. There's no law that says we have to do this right now."

She shook her head. "No. I want to. More than I've

ever wanted anything. I'm just nervous." She nibbled her lip. "It feel like…like I've never done this before."

He swallowed his anger and kept his face straight.

"I know it's silly, but…*he* never took this much care. Didn't look me in the face. Hell, he never took me from the front…" Her words trailed off and then she stiffened and continued. "I know this might seem like a stupid time to bring all this up, but I want you to know—you deserve to know—what this means to me."

Stunned. He froze. He'd known she'd had a rough four years, but that bastard never had proper sex with her? God… When he got his hands on that asshole…

"Don't look at me like that." She squirmed beneath him and gripped his arms tighter.

Evan took a deep breath and closed his eyes for a moment, long enough to get a grip on his emotions. *You're with Ashley now. What matters is her and making her feel special.*

He opened his eyes and found doubt in her furrowed brow. "I'm sorry." He kissed her gently. "I'm sorry for everything you endured. I promise to make the rest of your life so fantastic you won't remember what happened before me." He grinned. It might not have been completely real, but he meant it deep inside. "Ashley, will you let me be that man? The one who holds your hand for the rest of our lives? Will you let me claim you as my own?"

"Yes." Her word was a whisper. She exhaled slowly.

He settled over her, maintaining eye contact as he kissed her lips again and pressed into her tightness.

And God…so tight…

Ashley held his gaze, her eyes wider as he fully settled inside her.

He knew by the stretch she was in some discomfort, and he held steady, trying not to grit his teeth against the need to move.

Slow and easy, Evan.

He waited. She blinked. Her face relaxed, and then she smiled. "Move." She wiggled her ass beneath him.

That one word warmed his heart, reached inside him and assured him everything would be okay. He pulled out halfway and pressed back inside her warmth. This time he did grit his teeth. If he wasn't careful, he would come on the third stroke. "So tight, Ash… So wet…"

For a woman who thought she would need lube, she was sure slippery.

I did that… He beamed inside, proud she was his, proud he could affect her so thoroughly after everything she'd been through.

Evan held himself over his mate with shaky arms as he settled into a rhythm. He didn't let her break eye contact. He watched as her face relaxed and her eyes rolled repeatedly back each time he pressed forward.

A low groan escaped her lips, and she dug into his arms with her fingernails. He loved the feel of each indentation she marked him with. He hoped she scarred him for life, because mentally he was a goner. He might as well have the physical remnants of their mating to match.

She tightened around him and he knew she was close to coming. His cock surged tighter, if that was possible. When she tipped her head back and exposed her neck, he nestled the base of his cock firmly against her pussy and rocked. Her whole body went rigid as her orgasm swept through her. She shook. And her sweet tight pussy milked his cock until he couldn't hold back any longer.

He joined her into the abyss, teetering on the edge for one last second before he came. Drawn to be as close to Ashley as possible, he finally let his gaze leave her face, wrapped his arms under her arched chest, and tugged her close to his heart as he pulsed into her.

Evan nuzzled her neck, scenting her, commemorating this claiming with long slow inhales of her. She smelled so sweet, and he never wanted this moment to end.

Fearing he would squish her, he finally rolled to one side, taking her with him onto her side and not letting his cock slip from inside her warmth.

His vision returned to normal and he found her smiling at him. "I don't know what I was waiting for. That was…"

He chuckled. "Good?"

"Good doesn't begin to describe what we just did." She blushed and set her forehead against his chin. "My entire body is humming. I'm not sure when I'll regain the use of my arms and legs."

She wasn't kidding. Evan couldn't maneuver his limbs either. He hugged her tight against him, not wanting the moment to end.

Their hearts beat rapidly against one another, and Evan listened to the pulsing in his ear as they meshed as though proclaiming their joined rhythms were some indication of the completed claiming.

He could sense her calmness. She was relieved. Discovering she could indeed mate and enjoy the act relaxed her.

She wiggled from his clutches. "You're squeezing the breath out of me." She giggled, the sound music to his ears. He loved her laugh. It was rare.

He released her reluctantly, giving her a few inches between them. His cock slipped free.

"Thank you," she whispered, her face serious.

He chuckled. "I think I should be thanking you."

"Well, still. Thank you for showing me there's more to life…and sex…than I could have imagined. That was so very different from any previous experience there is no comparison. Damon Parkfield was not my mate. He did nothing for me and he led me to believe it was all my fault."

"It was not. I'm glad you can see that clearly. You're mine now and he'll never hurt you again." *Now I just have to find the bastard and make sure those words ring true.*

"You can't know that for sure, but I appreciate the sentiment." She glanced over her shoulder. "Do you have a bathtub in there?"

"Of course." He smiled. "I'll go run it for you. Hang tight a second." He pulled himself free of her warm skin and jerked the blanket from the foot of the bed to cover her.

She shivered as she snuggled under the cool sheets and curled onto her side, letting her eyes drift shut. A smile bigger than any he'd ever seen on her face took up residence. Her breaths slowed. Her mouth parted as she fell asleep.

He continued to stare down at her for long moments, watching her relaxed features, her glorious blonde curls, her soft cheeks flushed with their recent lovemaking. She needed sleep. He knew she hadn't slept well in months. Hell, years. The bath could wait.

Instead he eased his jeans from the bed and padded to the bathroom to dispose of the condom and clean himself up. He felt like a million tiny weights had been lifted from his shoulders. He walked lighter as he reentered the bedroom and tiptoed past his sweet mate.

He had so much work to do. The council was counting on him to plow through all that material in just a few days and then resume his search for one rogue wolf who may or may not be quite as rogue as previously believed.

Someone was giving that man drugs. Evan suspected there was an entire conspiracy of sorts behind the strange substance he'd been giving Ashley. Damon Parkfield was one small piece of a giant puzzle, but the man was the only lead Evan or The Council had so far. He needed to track that bastard down and tug on the rope that bound Damon to his supplier.

A chill crept up Evan's neck. He'd never been as sure as he was right then. His goal was clear and his motivation was strong. Until he found Damon and managed to get the man in custody, Ashley could never fully relax.

Heading to his office to resume his research, Evan held his head high. His cock still stood at attention and he wished he could spend the entire day lounging with his newly claimed mate, but as long as she was sleeping he had work to do.

Sitting around staring at her face in slumber wouldn't help solve the bizarre crime he had devoted himself to investigating.

CHAPTER 17

Two weeks later...

Evan reached for his phone as it buzzed against his thigh. He didn't take his eyes off the apartment he watched as he answered. "Harmon here." He hadn't glanced at the caller ID. That's how focused he was. Intent.

"Hey. This is David. Just checking in, boss." He chuckled. "Are you still on that secret mission? I mean don't worry about us back here at the office. We've got it covered."

"Oh, sorry. Guess it's been a few days since I checked in."

"Yes, I'd say six to be precise. Are you okay?"

"Yep." *I'll be better when I nail this bastard to the wall.* Evan was confident he had finally found Damon Parkfield. If Damon didn't emerge from the apartment Evan was facing in the next hour, Evan was going to pay him a visit. He'd rather get a visual first, but he wouldn't risk more than another hour of surveillance on the off chance Damon was onto him and fled again.

"Okay... I guess you aren't in your chatty mode. I'll let you get back to it then. No worries here. I have two men out on assignment and I'm manning the fort."

"Good. Thanks. David, I'm sorry. I'm knee deep right now. I appreciate you immensely and I will give you my undivided attention the moment I have the opportunity." Evan remained rigid. Poised. His leg bounced and his eyes burned from not blinking enough.

"Okay, boss. Later." David hung up.

Bless that man and all he did to hold the business together while Evan was away. Hiring him was one of the best decisions Evan had ever made. He knew he could count on David to run the office like a well-tuned engine.

Initially, Evan created his own PI company so he could be home and still have money coming in from the men he employed. Now that Evan was also employed by a much bigger fish with a hefty contract, he had no financial worries at all.

Evan glanced at his watch. It was still early in St. Louis. Hell, it was early in Virginia. Ashley would be sleeping at her parents' house. When he was out of town, she didn't stay at his place alone. Now *their* place.

He called her several times a day and he'd been gone six days this time. It wasn't ideal and she was growing weary. He could hear it in her voice. There was only so much a newly mated shifter could do to assure his woman when he wasn't in town more than a day at a time.

He couldn't blame her. He'd spent three glorious days making love to her sexy body and then took off for a job he couldn't discuss with her. Not a word. She had no idea he was hunting her own ex, nor that he'd been hired by The Head Council to do so. And besides, he wouldn't dare risk telling her anyway. He knew she'd freak out from fear or anger or both.

Nope. It was best to get this job done and then deal with the fallout. He prayed she would forgive his involvement.

Eyes still plastered to the apartment door, Evan knew his personal time limit was up. He had to move. He climbed out of the rental car and stretched his legs. A window sat to the right of the apartment entrance and he could have sworn he saw the curtain flutter.

That couldn't be good.

He moved quickly on achy legs. If that bastard saw him, he would flee so fast Evan wouldn't stand a chance. Damon couldn't be very smart in general, but he was sure astute when it came to running away from detection.

How the hell did that man always seem to be one step ahead of Evan? It made a chill run down his spine every time he thought about it. He'd never thought of himself as being very obvious in his investigations, but Damon's ability to detect him was bordering on eerie.

There were fifty yards between Evan and that apartment. The curtain moved again, definitively. Evan picked up his pace, but he had to circumvent several large shrubs and the railing that ran around the front of the building.

He was too late. The front door whipped open and Damon emerged. The man carried only a backpack, but he took off running in the opposite direction so fast Evan couldn't communicate with his legs to scramble.

Shit.

Evan ran, but Damon had a direct route around the end of the building. He disappeared from sight long before Evan could reach him.

By the time Evan rounded the corner, Damon was gone. Seconds. That man was fucking fast and always on alert. *Goddamn it.* Evan looked every direction. Nothing. He could have jumped in a car, ducked into another apartment. Hell, the bastard was so skinny he could be hiding behind a tree.

Evan stomped around the area, but he found nothing. Poof. As though the man had never been there. Finally, he gave up and headed for the apartment, furious with the way the man managed to get the upper hand. Evan's skin crawled. It seemed once again someone had tipped Damon off. There was no way Damon could be as astute as he seemed time and time again.

Evan stopped outside Damon's apartment and turned around. He held on to the frame of the door Damon had left open and looked around. Was someone watching *him*? It gave him the creeps.

Evan finally stepped inside, fear of what he might find niggling at the back of his neck. There was still no certainty Damon didn't have another woman by now. "Anyone home?"

No answer. Evan took his time entering anyway. He shut the door behind him, turned the deadbolt, and secured the chain lock. He was taking no chances with Parkfield. The man was so unpredictable there was no guarantee he wouldn't return and take Evan by surprise from behind.

The place was immaculate. No surprise there. Obviously the guy was type A the way he'd used Ashley as a slave to his house chores.

Evan began the tedious task of going through Damon's belongings. The man had left with only the sparse number of things he could carry. This was the first time Evan had caught him unaware enough to go through his belongings instead of finding the place wiped clean of all evidence.

He opened cabinets and drawers in the kitchen area first. Nothing. Plates, utensils, nothing out of the ordinary.

The refrigerator held only a few items—some milk, beer, lunch meat, condiments, not much else.

Next he stepped into the bedroom. There was only one. It was a small place. Kitchenette, living room, bedroom, bathroom. It wouldn't take Evan long to canvas the entire scene.

A small closet held only a few pairs of pants, shoes, shirts…

A dresser was half empty.

Fuck.

Evan spun around, wanting to throw the bedside

lamp across the room. He was that pissed. The man slipped through his fingers again, and he'd left nothing interesting. Angry now, Evan started tossing shit left and right. He flipped the mattress over.

He stomped into the living room and tore the couch cushions off. Even the fabric underneath them was clean. The only other piece of furniture in the room was an older-model TV. Evan couldn't imagine it worked. It sat on a rickety cheap stand.

Evan plopped down on the edge of the couch, not caring there was no longer a cushion to sit on. *Think.* He had to be missing something.

He pushed his hands into his hair. He needed to get control of his anger. He was a professional and he'd done enough jobs like this to know he wouldn't find a damn thing in his current state of mind.

He leaned back and stared at the ceiling, catching his breath. When he felt sufficiently calm, he let his gaze roam the room again.

End table. Nothing on it. Didn't the guy at least have a remote? It sure hadn't been between the couch cushions. He smirked as he lifted his gaze to the television once again. The stand was nothing more than a metal tray of sorts. He followed the electrical cord from where it dangled behind the TV to the wall.

And then he froze. He knew damn good and well no one could watch TV these days without cable or at least some sort of box to give access to channels. He bolted upright and reached the twenty-four inch in two steps.

He intended to pull it out from the wall to investigate behind it, but when he reached from above, hoping the wheeled cart would slide forward, the entire television teetered forward and crashed to the floor.

Evan jumped to avoid the glass. Except nothing broke. This was no ordinary TV. It weighed nothing. And its uselessness as a means of checking the local news was quickly revealed. It had a completely false front that didn't break when it hit the ground. Plexiglas he presumed.

The back fell off entirely in the fall to divulge not electronic components, but vials of drugs and syringes. *Bingo.*

Evan sprang into action. He ran back to the bedroom, found a duffle, and returned to fill it with the evidence. Thank God. This was headway.

He might not have captured the man himself, but at least he had the drugs. From his viewpoint, he had killed two birds. One, Damon no longer had the means to shoot up another woman. And two, the evidence could go a long way toward finding out who the supplier was and nailing the bigger fish.

In minutes, Evan was done. He shouldered the bag and slipped back out the door.

A half an hour later, he pulled into the airport. He wasn't stupid enough to cart the unknown drugs across the country by plane. He'd dropped that precious cargo off at FedEx first, overnighting it to The Council headquarters. Evan would beat the package, but at least by this time tomorrow he would have the strange substance safely in the hands of pack leaders.

Sure, he had the authority to carry the package on the plane, but the red tape would have been a huge hassle and he didn't want to deal with the delay. The quickest, easiest way to get himself and the drugs to Seattle was to separate himself from the duffle bag and get a move on.

A weight lifted from his shoulders, but not completely. He still cussed under his breath at losing Parkfield. That man was a slippery motherfucker. Evan knew neither he nor Ashley could sleep well until Damon was caught.

Evan had to wait forty-five minutes at the gate before boarding. He called Ashley as he slumped into an uncomfortable black chair in the terminal.

"Evan?"

"Hey, baby. How are you?"

"Good. When are you coming home?"

"Soon. I need to make another stop and then I'll be home for a few days." He hoped the trip to Seattle would be brief.

"You have to go out again so quickly?" Her voice was high-pitched. Stressed. He knew he was trying her patience with this case. If she only knew…

"Yeah. I'm sorry. As soon as I wrap this up I'll be able to work from home without nearly as much travel. But like I told you, this was a commitment I made and I have to keep it."

"I know." Her voice deflated as she spoke.

"Are you at your parents'?"

"Yeah."

"How's your schoolwork?"

"Going good. It's not like I have a lot of distractions." She giggled and his cock hardened at the sound. He loved the tinkle of her voice. It was unnatural for newly mated couples to separate like this. Fucking impossible. If he weren't so consumed with tracking this asshole, there was no way he would be able to concentrate on anything. As it was, he had to turn his brain off to the existence of Ashley by day.

By night he lay in random hotel rooms thinking of her sweet body and wishing she was next to him. Her scent lingered on his belongings, but after six days he was relying on memories.

"Have you been painting?"

"Yep." She sighed. "Come home quick, okay?"

"I'm on it. Promise. So close." *And yet so far…*

"I don't sleep as well when you aren't next to me." He could practically hear her biting her lip.

"I don't either, baby. I'm exhausted." That was the truth. He'd been exhausted for months ever since he'd first spotted her when he'd led her brother to her rescue.

A loud speaker in the terminal announced his flight. "I gotta go. My plane is boarding. I'll call you tonight."

"Okay. Be careful."

"Always."

~

Damon placed the usual call to the Romulus. He was out of breath and had only snagged a few items when he'd received the call that someone was on to him. Again.

Luckily, he'd grabbed the throw-away cell.

"Yes?" The deep voice that picked up on the first ring always answered this same way.

"I'm on the run."

"Did anyone see you?"

Damon paused. This was the first time he'd been almost caught. Should he fess up? Would the Romulus be mad?

Oh, what the fuck did he care anymore? Those bastards were making his life a living hell. He'd been perfectly fine, living alone with no other shifters for miles around until these fuckers had shown up promising the moon. In retrospect he should have realized when something sounded too good to be true, he should have listened to his brain. "Yes. Some asshole was already making his way to the front door. Your warning was a bit tardy this time."

Damon was weary, exhausted from fucking moving all the time and having to remain on alert. The Romulus insisted he had no other choice. It was unfortunate things hadn't gone as planned with Ashley, but *these things* went south sometimes.

No shit, motherfuckers.

A long exhale came from the other end of the line.

"Listen. This is not my fault; it's yours. I've about had it with your shit. So don't fucking sigh your deep breath at me, you asshole. I'm two seconds from turning your asses in and myself too for some peace and quiet. Even prison sounds like a walk in the park about now." Damon paced the short distance back and forth in the cheap motel room he'd rented for the night. He couldn't afford more with the cash he'd had on him.

"Calm down," the deep voice demanded.

"Calm down? Do you realize how many times you've said that in the last five years? Too many to count, you son of a bitch. I'm going to give you about one week to put an end to this mess and then I'm going it alone."

"You know you can't do that. If you so much as breathe wrong, your ass will land in a place worse than prison for the rest of your life." The guy paused before continuing. "Now, sit down and take some deep breaths. We've told you before how serious this is. The only choice you have is to ride out the search party and then we'll have you settled again in no time with a new mate."

"This is one very long ride, buddy."

"I know, but that two-bit PI can't follow you forever. He'll give up soon." The man chuckled, a maniacal sound that made Damon's blood freeze. "He'll have to go home soon before Ashley loses it and dumps his ass."

Damon swallowed. His vision blurred. "What the fuck did you say?"

Silence. "Sorry, man. Thought you knew."

"That jackass following me is fucking my mate?"

"It seems that way. But who cares? She was a bitch anyway, right? Let him have her. We have a lead on someone much more acquiescent for you."

Damon took a deep breath. His blood pounded again now, thawing and then boiling as his anger rose.

"Listen, just hang tight. We'll make arrangements for you to be moved soon. Stay where you are and don't let anyone unnecessary see you. Got it?"

"Sure. Whatever." Damon barely listened to that last

part. All he could think about was why Ashley's new partner was following him. Fear climbed up his spine, making his hand shake until he nearly dropped the cell phone.

I'll kill that bastard, and Ashley too while I'm at it.

The line went dead and Damon dropped the cell on the cheap old comforter covering the cheaper older mattress that dipped in the middle. He ran a hand through his hair.

On top of everything else, he hadn't managed to point out that the drug paraphernalia had gotten left behind in his haste this time. He'd never left anything behind. He'd hidden it so well, even an FBI agent would have had trouble finding it.

Thank God he'd had an escape plan. He'd watched that man sitting in his car after the Romulus had contacted him. When the man had exited the vehicle and headed straight for Damon's hovel, Damon had praised the Lord he'd already made arrangements for a hiding place.

All he'd had to do was dash around the corner. In seconds he had himself locked in a supply room at the end of the building. He'd picked the lock in the middle of the night the first day he'd arrived. It was perfect. No apartment employee had used the room since, so no one knew it was unlocked yet.

The moment he'd entered, he'd easily turned the deadbolt, sequestering himself from whoever was chasing him before the guy circled the building. Hopefully the bastard assumed Damon had driven away or been picked up.

CHAPTER 18

Evan opened the front door of his home, turned toward the alarm panel, and pushed the buttons to deactivate. He set his briefcase on the small table and dropped his duffle inside the front room. He pushed the door closed and reset the alarm. His intent was to grab a quick shower and then race to Ashley's parents'. Instead, he froze in his spot. He'd known the place would smell of his mate. They'd made love many times in the last few weeks in that confined space. But he hadn't been prepared for the overwhelming, knee-buckling, enticing scent that made him want to forego the shower and turn around to get back in the car.

He closed his eyes and inhaled long and slow, knowing if he didn't hurry, he would lose his resolve to shower and change. The least he could do was show up looking presentable. Flying always made him feel grungy no matter how long ago he'd showered.

When he opened his eyes again, they landed on the most delicious sight he'd ever seen.

Ashley. Even in the dim evening glow from outside, without turning on the lights, he spotted her immediately.

No wonder the place smelled so strongly of her pheromones. She was there, in the flesh. He blinked to be sure she wasn't an apparition and then dashed across the room to where she stood leaning on the frame to the hallway.

She giggled as he lifted her off the floor and squeezed her against his length. His cock jumped to attention at this new turn of events. The fellow had been told to wait at least another hour and suddenly had received the new information that its prison sentence would be lifted a bit earlier than expected.

"You're here alone?" He glanced from side to side. Surely someone brought her here. And she wouldn't have stayed alone.

"Yes." She kissed his lips. "My mother dropped me off."

He raised an eyebrow. "I'm so glad." She was getting braver. He kissed her back, his lips smashing into hers as he backed her up against the wall. He needed more of her, craved her like a drug.

And she responded, tugging at his shirt until she had it over his head.

"I was going to take a shower…" His voice trailed off as she nibbled on his neck. The timid sweet little mate he'd claimed just weeks ago was no longer quite so shy.

"No. Don't," she muttered against his skin. "I love how you smell. I don't want you to wash it away." She licked a bold path down his chest until she flicked her tongue over his nipple.

His already hardening cock went full speed ahead, jamming against his pants and making him very uncomfortable.

It didn't last long. Ashley slunk down and popped the button on his khakis. She lowered the zipper slow enough to send a shiver down his spine.

He planted his hands on the wall above her, bracing himself and hoping to keep from falling.

She pulled on the sides of his pants and lowered them to the ground. His cock sprung free as though sighing with gratitude. "Baby…" He wouldn't last long like this with her torturing him. When she set her palms on his shins and then smoothed her hands up the length of his legs, he moaned.

She gripped his thighs and squeezed, her face inches from his bobbing cock. On her knees in front of him… He held his breath. She hadn't given him a blowjob yet. And he hadn't mentioned it. He didn't know what she'd gone through with her ex, but if she'd been forced to suck him off, Evan wanted no part in that reenactment.

She didn't flinch, however. Her gaze landed on his dick and she released his legs to tentatively stroke the length with both hands. "So smooth," she muttered.

He watched as a pearl of come leaked from the tip.

Ashley held his cock with one hand and her sweet tongue darted out to lick away his come.

Evan's knees threatened total collapse. He curled his fingers on the wall as though he could get some sort of purchase against the smooth surface.

"I missed you." Ashley sucked his head into her mouth before he could respond. She moaned around the tip and then released him with a soft pop. "I love that I do this to you."

All the blood ran to his dick, leaving him speechless, unable to send messages to his mouth.

She sucked him in again and then licked the length clear to the base. With one hand she held him steady. With the other she caressed his balls. "Can I touch these?"

He cleared his throat, unsure if he could articulate anything to the affirmative. "Yes, gently…"

She fondled his sac with her dainty fingers, barely touching him. And then she reached behind him with that free hand and grasped his ass. Her mouth sunk low on his cock, leaving him lightheaded. She sucked, hard, and then pulled almost off before repeating the same action.

Evan finally let go of the wall with one hand to weave his fingers into her hair. "Baby, you have to stop that…"

She let him fall out of her mouth and looked up at him. "Did I do something wrong?" The way she batted her eyes told him she knew damn well she had done nothing wrong.

He grasped her head with both hands and eased her up to standing. He kissed her forehead and then buried his nose in her soft hair. She smelled so fucking good. It was his turn to snack…

With amazing dexterity, Evan managed to kick his shoes off and then stepped on the legs of his pants until they came away also, taking his underwear with them. "I'm decidedly less dressed than you." He lifted her chin and took her mouth in a kiss, delving into her sweet cavern and letting his tongue dance with hers. He swallowed her moan.

As he continued to nibble her mouth, he backed them down the hall. Expertly, he found the bedroom in the dark, kicked the door ajar with his foot and proceeded across the floor.

Ashley held his biceps with both arms and didn't come up for air until he hit the edge of the bed, jarring them both.

She giggled when her belly ran into his cock. He moaned in response. "Take your clothes off, baby. I need you."

She stepped back. The blinds were open, providing plenty of light from the moon for him to see her sultry expression as she unbuttoned her shirt and let it drift to the ground. She teased him by shimmying out of her pants and then stood before him in nothing but sexy black lingerie.

"You've been shopping." He smoldered as he watched her sway toward him once again. Her firm high breasts were accented by the black lace that barely covered her nipples.

"Online, but yes."

"I like it." He reached out to stroke the upper swell of her breast with one finger.

Goose bumps rose in the wake of his touch, and he traced over them as she shivered.

"And I like your response even more."

"I can't get enough of you. How about if you stay in town for a while this time?" She didn't whine, but she did stick out her bottom lip in a fake pout. "I might be able to make it worth your while."

"I'm quite certain you could, baby. And I wish I wasn't held to this contract. It'll be over soon." *If that weasel would sit still a minute.* It was amazing how astute Parkfield was considering what an ass he was.

Ashley surprised Evan by shoving him onto the bed, climbing onto his lap, and straddling him. His cock tucked neatly against her thong, the lace barely covering the soft triangle of hair above her clit.

He fell onto his back when she pushed him again playfully, and he scooted them both into the center of the bed. She'd never been this brazen, and he liked it. She was coming around.

He hoped he could add to her experiences by emulating what she'd just done to him.

She squealed as he swung them both around, holding her straddling his waist. When he had them lined up with the top of the bed, he looked into her eyes. "Grab the headboard, Ash." She eyed him suspiciously, narrowing her gaze. "And scoot forward." He nudged her hips and urged her to kneel closer to his mouth, straddling his lips.

"What…?" The word faded as he used both hands to grip her ass cheeks and pulled her closer to his mouth. He held her steady and sucked her essence through the lace barrier.

She trembled. "Oh God."

Evan grinned into her wet pussy and reached

around her thighs from behind her to stroke through her folds. He toyed with the thin strip of lace between her cheeks, dragging it back and forth through her pussy lips.

"Evan..."

Finally, he pulled the thong aside and exposed her clit to his mouth. He flicked his tongue over the tight nub several times and then sucked it between his lips.

"Evan," she shouted, louder than the first time.

This was perfect. She was on top, giving the illusion of being in complete control. He knew she wouldn't balk at many things as long as she was on top of him. He'd learned that quickly. She was also comfortable in missionary position. He doubted he'd ever take her from behind. It seemed that was Damon's only style. If that was Evan's only concession in life, he would die a very happy man.

Evan flattened his tongue against her clit and pressed a finger into her slit. She was so fucking wet. His cock twitched. He needed her over him, enveloping him. Now.

He released her from his mouth, making her moan in frustration.

"Oh, God. No..." Her eyes shot wide when she muttered that last word, and his chest swelled at her wantonness. "I..." She bit her lip and let her gaze slip to her pussy, unable to make eye contact with him.

"I know, baby. I want you to come on my cock. I love how your pussy grips me, pulsing around my length."

Her gaze shot back to him, still wide as though she couldn't believe how blatant he spoke.

"Scoot down." He pressed her hips. As she released the headboard, he tugged on her thong. She had to lift one leg over him to remove it, and then she resumed her spot, scrambling to straddle him again. She nestled against him, trapping his cock flat against his belly between her pussy lips. Sitting upright, she smoothed her hands over his chest.

His breathing hitched. He needed her now. She was taking her sweet time.

She pinched his nipples, making him buck into her touch. "Just making sure I'm not the only one on the edge here."

"Never, baby. Never." He lifted her torso, freeing his cock to line up with her entrance. And then he eased her down until she was fully seated.

Like a swan, she arched her entire body over him, her head thrown back, elongating her neck. Her breasts stood high and firm still encased in her bra, and he cupped them both in his hands. He pinched her nipples through the lace, imitating her own action seconds ago, and then he reached for the center clasp and popped it open to release her chest to his gaze. He drew the straps down her arms and tossed the lingerie aside.

She didn't lift up yet. Instead she ground her clit against him. And she moaned. When her face came back into view, she smiled. "I love you." Her cheeks flushed a deep red. It was the first time she'd said those three words, and he'd waited, biting his tongue for weeks, not wanting to scare her by repeating them to her after the first time he'd declared his love.

"God, Ashley. I love you too. More than anything in

the world." He grazed his fingers down her belly and then between her legs. He held her open farther, if that was possible, and clasped her clit between his thumbs. "Pinch your nipples for me, baby."

She paused a moment, but her sweet fingers lifted at his encouragement and she squeezed both breasts, pinning her nipples between her first two fingers on each side. She arched again, and he rolled her clit between his thumbs.

"I'm gonna come." She rocked back and forth.

"That's the plan. You're so sexy," he whispered. "So fucking sexy." His cock demanded attention, confined without movement. But he wanted her to come first so he could both watch her face and feel her pulse around him. Those were the moments he lived for.

A long moan escaped her lips and she bucked into him harder, her hands gripping her breasts firmly. The moment she tipped over the edge, he watched her face intently. She threw her head back again and he couldn't see her eyes, but her jaw hung open and she held her breath, her entire body freezing in place as she rode the waves of her orgasm.

When her pulsing finally slowed, she lowered her gaze to his. "That never ceases to amaze me," she muttered. She leaned forward, releasing her chest to set her hands on his pecs. And then she lifted partway off his cock, only to lower languidly back over him. She watched his expression intently as he had just done to her.

His vision blurred as she rode him. She moved faster

with each return. His cock buried so deep inside her in this position. *So fucking hot.*

He grazed his hands up and down her back, but he couldn't really feel anything in his fingers. Couldn't enjoy her smooth flesh at the moment. All his concentration was centered on her tight pussy around his cock.

When she leaned forward and rested on her hands on both sides of his face, taking his mouth in a kiss, the change in position made his cock swell harder. He came, deep inside his mate, his come jutting out in forceful streams that seemed more intense than any other time they'd been together.

He squeezed his eyes shut, enjoying the feel of her warmth wrapped around him, her lips licking and nibbling around a mouth he had no control over for several moments.

Finally she stilled, leaving him lodged deep inside her. His cock still jerked. His heart raced as he regained the use of his lips and kissed her back.

She was so wet. Her moisture coated him more than he could ever remember. He squirmed beneath her, loving the increased sensitivity.

She moaned. And then both their eyes shot wide at the same time.

"Shit." She didn't move, but she glanced down. "We forgot the condom."

He swallowed. "Yes. I guess I got carried away. I'm sorry." He knew she couldn't get pregnant right now, but she hadn't fully grasped the ability to detect such a thing yet.

She relaxed. "I don't know why I care. I love having you bare inside me and I'll prove to you I can't get pregnant." She smiled as though she knew a secret.

"Well, you can't get pregnant today. You're not ovulating. But, I still didn't mean to scare you."

"I don't care. I'd be over the moon if I really conceived, so you can stop using those dumb condoms any time you want."

"Are you sure?" He stroked her back. "It's not the kind of thing you want to do to prove a point. Besides, I'll win this bet."

"Scared?" She lifted one brow.

"Hell, no. You're my life, Ashley. I'd welcome as many babies as you can handle."

"And if I don't ever conceive?"

He didn't know the words to comfort her. "Then we'll be the most rested couple around for eternity."

She swatted his chest and then snuggled against him. "When do you have to leave again?"

"Not sure. A few days." He reflected on his trip to Seattle while she fell asleep against him.

The Council had received the package and sent half the contents to a team of medical professionals they'd hired on the side. Since none of them were sure what sort of drug they were dealing with, they'd privately contracted members of the shifter community, in case the strange derivative of Rohypnol with traces of Scopolamine was something unknown to the strictly human population. If word got out that someone was using illegal substances to control women... He didn't want to ponder that possibility.

So far Ashley was the only known victim. Other missing women were suspect, but there was no proof other than the blood tests done on Ashley over twenty-four hours after her rescue.

The find was a goldmine. Almost as good as nailing Damon Parkfield himself would be.

CHAPTER 19

The sun shone bright when Ashley wandered into the kitchen the next morning. Evan stood at the stove, the scent of bacon drifting through the entire house. That's what had lured her from a deep sleep. Wearing only a T-shirt she'd grabbed from Evan's drawer, she slunk up behind him and wrapped her arms around his waist.

He didn't flinch. Of course. It wasn't as though she could have hidden her approach.

She smiled and breathed deeply of his masculinity.

He reached around and wrapped an arm around her, drawing her up to his side. He kissed the top of her head. "Did you sleep well?"

"You know I did." She lifted her gaze. She knew she was a mess, her uncombed hair tousled around her head. But he didn't care. His gaze was only filled with admiration. "I always sleep soundly when you're in town." She poked his stomach before continuing. "I don't sleep well when you aren't home."

"I'm working on fixing that." He lifted bacon from

the skillet and set several lengths on a paper towel with his spatula. Without releasing her from his side, he stretched across her to grab a carton of eggs. Somehow he managed to open the carton and crack several eggs into the pan with one hand.

"You're good with your hands." She bit her lip as he slipped the one around her waist under the shirt to cup her ass.

"I'm glad you feel that way." He flipped the eggs quickly and gave them a few moments before removing them to settle them next to the bacon.

And then he turned toward her, took her face in both hands, and kissed her senseless. "Good morning."

She squeezed her legs together. She was insatiable around him. Every time he was in town they had sex at all hours of the day and night. It was surprising she ever got enough sleep. But when she slept with him, she slept hard.

The kiss deepened and she melted into his embrace. Emboldened, she stepped out with one leg and straddled his thigh, immediately rubbing her naked clit against his muscles. Evan released her face and lowered his hands to her hips. He spun them both around without breaking the kiss and lifted her in one quick movement up onto the kitchen island. With a swift tug, he swept her shirt over her head and tossed it away at her back.

She flinched when a soft crash occurred behind her, and she twisted around to find his briefcase had fallen onto the floor. It could wait. She needed more contact with Evan before she combusted.

Evan was unfazed by the disturbance. He settled between her legs and took a nipple between his lips. When he bit down gently, she writhed. "Evan..." She squeezed his shoulders, but couldn't keep from bucking her chest farther into his mouth. "Please..." She'd gone from zero to infinity in two seconds flat.

He reached between her outstretched legs and stroked a finger through her pussy. She nearly came off the countertop. And then he flipped his palm face up and reached inside her with two fingers. His thumb landed on her clit and pressed hard as he rubbed her G-spot. His mouth continued to assault her chest, nibbling first one breast and then the other until she couldn't think straight. So many neurons all firing at once. Through her fog, she focused on her channel. She was always lost when he applied pressure to both her most sensitive areas at once. And this morning was no exception.

She tightened around him, amazed by how easily he could play her, make her hum.

The second he squeezed his fingers upward against the tight wall of her pussy, she came. Her entire body stiffened as she rocked against his hand. He kept stroking her, easing gradually until she finally collapsed forward, setting her chin on his head, trying to catch her breath.

"God, Evan. You have some sort of magic power over my body. It's...disconcerting."

"It's beautiful. I wouldn't have it any other way." He lifted from her chest, forcing her to hold her head up on her own, somehow.

"It feels so damn good every time I come, but it's not as satisfying as having you inside me." She tipped her head to one side. "I never feel quite...fulfilled." She was being coy, but she also knew it wasn't necessary. No way was he going to waste the huge erection that bobbed in front of her. And no way was she going to let him.

He wore pajama bottoms low on his hips, but his cock jutted out the top now, the head covered in his pre-come.

She wrapped her legs around his waist and easily pushed his pants down with her feet until they fell to the ground. "Oops."

The word died on her lips and she yelped when he lifted her off the island and settled her directly on his cock. She slid down his length quickly, filling herself to the hilt.

"You're going to be the death of me, Ashley. You humble me every day." He stepped around the island, keeping himself embedded inside her. The only sign he was winded was the gritting of his teeth and she imagined that was to keep from coming, not because he strained to hold her up.

She squealed again when her back hit the cold surface of the refrigerator. She bucked her ass forward to avoid the cold, but only managed to force Evan deeper.

He held her waist. She gripped his shoulders. And then he made love to her up against the shiny chrome. It didn't matter that they were standing naked in the kitchen. It didn't matter that the floor was scattered with papers that had fallen out of his briefcase. It didn't matter that the blinds were open on the tiny window above the sink.

Ashley glanced at all these things, and then she let her gaze land on Evan's. And she held it the entire time he made love to her. Long luxurious strokes inside her that reached to her soul. She came again. She always did. And he filled her as he had last night with his own orgasm.

Evan took two steps back until he leaned against the island. He slid down the short wall of tile until he sat on the ground, Ashley still nestled over his cock.

It amazed her once again how strong he was.

She set her cheek on his shoulder, her face turned out to catch her breath. Her vision cleared as her blood began to circulate through the rest of her body. She stared absently at the scattered papers on the floor. Moments passed before she realized what she was seeing.

Damon Parkfield's name was on nearly every page. It stood out like a knife stabbing her in the gut. She jerked upright and lifted herself off Evan's lap in one movement.

As she knelt in the mess, her fingers shook. She reached for the first page she could grab and held it up.

Drugs... Conspiracy... Damon... Parkfield... Must be caught... Dangerous... Alive...

Her head swam. Her arm shook. She yanked her gaze toward Evan who had yet to open his eyes. "What is this?" Her voice was high pitched. Loud. She scared herself.

He flinched. His eyes went wide when he realized what she held, and he jerked the pages from her hand. "Work. You weren't supposed to see that."

She scrambled to stand and back away. "I gathered that. What the fuck, Evan? Are you investigating Damon?" She backed into the same cold surface of the refrigerator, this time glad for the cool metal that helped bring her brain back to full function.

Evan reached for her, pushing the papers out of sight with one hand.

"Is that what you've been doing this entire time? Hunting that asshole?" She wiggled from his reach and stepped away toward the hall. She shook her head. Her entire body quivered. She spun to face him. "Evan, no. You have to stop this. It's madness. I'm working really hard to put this behind me and you're out there every day hunting my ex?"

"Ash, I'm doing a job." He stood, his shoulders slumped. The pages he held fell from his hands and fluttered to the ground.

Her world turned upside down. She felt betrayed somehow. "How long have you been doing this?"

"Ashley…"

"How long?" she shouted.

He exhaled and lowered his gaze. "Since the day we rescued you."

She sucked in a deep breath. Her head swam. She needed to sit down. She turned and stumbled down the hall for the bedroom. With nothing else to do and no way to hold herself upright, she scrambled onto the bed and under the covers, curling up into a ball.

Evan was there one second behind her. He had the good sense not to touch her, but he sat on the edge of the bed inches from her frame. She didn't look at him directly. Her gaze locked onto his knee where it bent close to her face.

"Ash, I'm sorry. At first..." He paused. "At first I wanted to kill that bastard for what he did to you. I was working alone. I wasn't being paid. That's when I opened my own business and hired other people to work for me. It brought in enough income to sustain my...obsession.

"And then I met you...well, for the second time...at Josh's house. But you weren't ready and...I kept looking for Parkfield."

She interrupted him. "Well, you have to stop. I can't stand it. Let it go." She sat up, taking the sheet with her and squeezing it against her chest. "I don't want him in our lives." A shiver racked her body. "It's revolting to think you've become so obsessed with him. Even I don't give him that much energy."

Evan lowered his gaze. "I can't."

"What do you mean, you can't. Yes, you can. Just stop. Let it go. Stay here with me. If you're worried about my safety, the danger I face increases incrementally when you leave me. Do *not* go back out there. It's over."

He shook his head and raised his gaze. "I'm sorry, Ashley. It's not over. In fact, it's just begun. I found him this week. He ran. I didn't manage to catch him, but what I did get was his stash of drugs. That's what I've been handling. I'm not working for myself anymore. I work for The Head Council in Seattle. They contracted me to find Damon. I spent the day there yesterday handing over the drugs I found for analysis. This problem is potentially bigger than Damon Parkfield. The Council doesn't believe he works alone.

"I don't either. He isn't smart enough. Someone is supplying him. It has to be stopped. There are… others…" His voice trailed off as she watched him.

"Other what?"

"Missing people. Mostly women. What if someone else is being held like you were?" He shook his head. "It doesn't matter. I'm not trying to guilt you into supporting me. I have a contract with The Council. I'm not at liberty to walk away."

Ashley leaned back and let her body flop onto the mattress. *Fuck.* "I feel like you lied to me." The room suddenly seemed cold. She shook with anger and frustration, but she had her voice level under control and her brain was coming to life.

"I'm so sorry. I would never intentionally do anything to hurt you in any way. This got…out of my control and then I hoped I could wrap up the entire mess without worrying you with the details."

"Worrying me?" She twisted her head to see his face. "I'm fucking scared out of my mind. This doesn't constitute worry, Evan."

He set a hand on her thigh, but she pulled away, not ready for his touch. Damn him.

Silence pierced the room, deafening her. As if on cue, Evan's phone beeped where he'd left it next to the bed. He snatched it up while she stiffened. Even that little sound made her hold her breath.

He read a text and then lifted sorrowful eyes toward her. "I have to go back to Seattle this evening. The toxicology results are back."

"Now? You're going to leave again? Just like that?" She shook her head. "I can't do this, Evan. My plate is full with my own sanity. I can't add worrying about you to the list of daily activities. Do you not understand what that would do to me?"

"I do." His chest heaved as she watched. He ran his hands through his hair until it stood on end. "Ashley, it's not that simple. It's a job now. I'm under obligation to complete the task."

Ashley scrambled from the other side of the bed and rounded on him, leaving him sitting there as she stormed into the bathroom and slammed the door behind her.

She flipped on the water to the huge luxurious tub she'd already sat in many times. Maybe a soak would clear her mind and relax her enough to keep from screaming. What the hell was the matter with him?

She stepped into the tepid water before it was warm enough. She sat on the bottom as it filled, the cool water matching her emotional state. As the water rose and heated, her anger began to abate.

She leaned back against the wall of the tub. *It's his job. Get a grip.*

She stiffened to consider him out there searching for the asshole who essentially held her hostage for four years, if not physically, at least psychologically.

Deep breaths. In. Out. In... Out...

She closed her eyes as she calmed. There was another way she could look at this situation. Instead of acting out of fear and anger, she could be elated that her mate cared so much about her that he would do anything to ensure her safety, including risk his own life... She groaned and sunk deeper into the water.

Was she being unreasonable? Perhaps.

She dumped floral-scented bubbles into the tub in the stream of water and then flipped the knobs off. The fragrance had been a gift from her brother's mate, Samantha. She claimed it would soothe. And she'd been right. Ashley did in fact calm down, her heart rate slowing as she rationalized her situation.

She hated what Evan was doing, but her reasons were based on fear. She did have to consider everything he'd said. If there were other women out there being manipulated and cajoled with the same drug, it had to be stopped.

She twisted her neck when Evan opened the door. "Can I come in?"

"Yes." She glanced down. Only her head was visible now, the bubbles covering the rest of her from the neck down.

He sat on the edge of the tub and trailed his fingers through the bubbles. "I'm truly sorry, baby."

"I know." She sounded calmer, even to her own ears. "I am too."

He lifted his gaze to hers.

She grabbed his hand from under the water. "Come in with me?"

A smile spread across his face. "May I?"

"I insist. I need you wrapped around me." She scooted forward as he dropped his pajama pants once again.

He slid in behind her, and she settled against his chest. "Sorry I freaked out. I'm scared." She took a deep breath. "But you're right. You have to stop this before it happens to anyone else."

He ran his palms down her arms and twined his fingers with hers, wrapping both sets of their arms around her middle. He kissed her temple. "I promise I'm taking every precaution I can. I hate the thought of you worrying about me."

"I know."

"I'll only be in Seattle this time. I lost the trail on Parkfield again. My work is to concentrate on the drugs for now. We need to know who is supplying them and put an end to it."

"That could take a long time."

"It could. I won't deny that. But we'll cross one bridge at a time."

She relaxed into his huge frame, exhaling. "I hate it, but I'm selfish when it comes to you. I want you with me."

"And I don't like being apart from you either, baby." He kissed her temple. "It breaks my heart, especially since you can't stay alone in our house while I'm gone."

The way he said "our" house warmed her. Nothing was simply his anymore. They were completely intertwined. One. "I'm getting better every day. You're largely responsible for that."

"I'm so glad." He squeezed her tighter. "I'll make every trip as brief as possible. I promise. Bear with me while I sort through this mess."

She nodded. Tears slipped from her eyes. They weren't purely from sadness. They were a mixture of emotions that flooded her body and spilled out of her eyes. She was so blessed to have Evan in her life, to know a true mating was something she never expected. It saddened her when he was away. But she had to admit fear was never far from her mind. He made her feel safe. And that safety was not something she took for granted.

CHAPTER 20

At nine o'clock sharp the following morning, Evan entered the Seattle offices of The Head Council. The head elder, Jerard, whom he'd met with now on several occasions, ushered him into a conference room. The man shut the door with soft snick and then pulled out a large file folder. They were not short on paperwork at this office…

Jerard took a seat across from Evan and spread out a few pages so they faced Evan. "This is the toxicology report. We are very concerned, to say the least. Our experts tell us this is indeed a blend of Rohypnol and Scopolamine and it's not something available in any human market that we can tell. It was undoubtedly created by shifters for use on shifters."

Evan glanced down at the pages in front of him.

Jerard continued. "What concerns us most is the sheer quantity of what you brought in. If a rogue wolf shifter like Damon Parkfield can get his hands on that much of the drug, how many others have it? How widespread is this problem? Mr. Parkfield doesn't appear to be a man of means so how is he funding the habit?"

"God." Evan had feared all this, but hearing it firsthand was still stunning. "Most of these numbers mean nothing to me, I must admit, sir." He pointed to a long list of ingredients and what he assumed were percentages of each that comprised the drug.

"I didn't suspect they would." Jerard smiled. "They don't mean anything to me either. But the medical team wrote these reports yesterday and raised serious red flags. They're injecting lab rats today to see what affect the drugs have on the animals. It's hard to say what the combination of these ingredients might do to a human. Ms. Rice is the only know recipient and by the time we got her blood sample there were only traces of this left in her system.

"Since the only evidence we can use to deduce the effects are testimonies from Ashley, we have very little to work with. What we need is to locate others who might be affected and run blood tests. Of course this is a huge undertaking since we wouldn't want anyone to know about our work."

"Yes, it would be best to keep this under wraps for now," Evan agreed.

Jerard glanced down at the papers. He spread his palms on the table. "It seems the purpose of the drugs is to control women. Maybe they used Ashley as an experiment? Maybe she wasn't the first victim. But why?"

Evan had no answer and Jerard's question was undoubtedly rhetorical.

"Tracking down this asshole Parkfield and actually capturing him would help significantly—if we can get him to rat out the chain of command. However, assuming we don't find him fast enough, we think it might be better to start locating other victims. Would you agree?"

Evan nodded. "It seems like a good plan."

"I'm going to hire another investigator to resume the tracking of Parkfield. The guy's seen your face. We need a new mole out there that he won't suspect." Jerard lifted another file. Evan presumed it contained information on the new investigator.

"As much as I hate to agree, you're probably right." Evan narrowed his gaze and shook his head. "I don't think it's me who's tipping off Parkfield, however. There is no way that man is intelligent enough nor astute enough to be watching for me with special binoculars or something twenty-four-seven. He'd be exhausted. I've been thinking," *especially since chasing Damon down at his apartment*, "and I think someone else is tipping him off."

Jerard took a deep breath and nodded. "I agree. That's why I'm meeting with you alone this morning. I believe firmly there's an insider, in this building in fact, who informs Parkfield when to run." He glanced down and then back up, straightening his spine. "As much as I hate to admit it, I think we should stop meeting here, and I'm not going to involve the other head elders in our progress for a while. I can't be sure who to trust.

"I'm only going to share information with Steven Wightman for now. I want someone else to be aware of the situation and our plans, but I'm keeping it to a minimum. I've known Steven all his life. If I've misjudged his loyalty then there's no hope for me." He gave a wry smile, but it wasn't sincere. He wasn't altogether kidding.

"Damn." This was fucking huge.

"Yes, I'm betting someone with access to our paperwork, computers, and intel is staying one step ahead of you. Perhaps the phones are tapped. Hell, the room could be bugged for all I know."

Evan shivered and couldn't keep from glancing around.

"All the more reason not to meet here again. We need to stop the paper trail and keep all correspondence on secure lines. I don't think we can afford to take any chances. As much as I hate to think a member of my own staff is involved in something this dirty, the evidence suggests I must face the facts."

"It would seem that way, sir." Evan gripped the table, running his fingers under the edge as though he might bump into a bug.

"So switching gears, I'd like you to start investigating all the leads we have concerning other possible victims."

Evan lifted an eyebrow. That would mean he went in a whole other direction, no longer responsible for Damon or the drugs. Ashley would be pleased with that little tidbit of information. "All right, sir."

"There are at least a dozen, and possibly more, women whose families aren't completely convinced of the legitimacy of their matings. And that's just the ones who've contacted us. There could be more."

"Jeez." It was hardly conceivable to think someone in the shifter community was supplying experimental drugs to that many men.

"And, Evan, another thing. Don't limit your research to women. I've seen a few cases where men might be involved."

Evan jerked his head up. "Men?"

Jerard nodded. "It's possible that Ashley's case was an anomaly. Maybe her body reacted stronger than others to the drug. Or perhaps she was given a different combination. It's hard to say. But there could be women, and men, out there whose symptoms aren't so readily obvious. Perhaps they don't know they're receiving anything mind altering.

"Ashley's report states that although she was dazed and found herself too agreeable for large chunks of time, the only way she knew for sure she was drugged was because of the method—injections. Maybe others are receiving dosages in another form, possibly unbeknownst to them."

"Is that likely?"

"Well, the examiner I spoke to last night said there was no particular reason he could see that the ingredients in his study couldn't just as easily be produced in a pill form or a powder that could be stirred into a drink. Odorless and difficult to detect, like Rohypnol."

"Then why go to all the complication of administering Ashley the shots?"

Jerard leaned on his elbows. "Because if Damon was already doing so, there was no need to begin to hide anything from Ashley. She was already docile and compliable to him, so he had no reason to switch. The syringe version is cheaper and easier to obtain."

"What a cluster fuck. Pardon my language, sir." Evan flinched as he spoke.

"I couldn't have stated it better myself." Jerard sat back, grinning. "Now, let's address another issue."

"What's that, sir?"

"Since taking on this project you've mated with Ashley."

"That's true. Is that a problem?" Evan steadied himself by gripping his knees under the table as he gazed at Jerard. Matings were obvious to others. There was no keeping things like that a secret. Ralph Jerard and his entire office would have scented the distinction the first time Evan had entered the office after mating.

Jerard smiled. "Not for me. But I bet your mate isn't too pleased with you being gone all the time."

"No." Evan's ears burned, but he needed to tell the head elder about yesterday morning. He felt an obligation to disclose what happened when his papers spilled from his briefcase. "And in fact, sir, she's rather pissed. Unfortunately, she knows what I'm working on. It wasn't intentional. But yesterday morning we had a little incident with my research falling out of my briefcase, and she figured out I was tracking Parkfield when she stooped to pick it up. I'm terribly sorry for the indiscretion."

Would the elder be pissed about this development?

Apparently not. The man grinned wide. "I bet she was fuming." He sat back and crossed his arms.

"That's putting it mildly," Evan muttered.

"Well, I can't blame her. She's been through hell and back. The last thing she needs is her mate traipsing all over the world searching for bad guys in dangerous situations."

"That's pretty much what she said."

"Well, here's what I think." Jerard leaned forward again. "The legwork on many of these cases is extensive. You've proven time and again that you're a genius when it comes to locating missing people, even if you do have butterfingers when it comes to bringing them in." He chuckled. "I propose a new plan. How about if you do the legwork from home and we send others out to do the fieldwork?"

Evan swallowed his excitement. He could think of nothing better. Ashley would be so relieved. "Excellent plan. Ashley will thank you immensely. And I do have men who work for me that could be at our disposal if you need guys to do the field work."

"I'll keep that in mind. But, it may be that we're venturing into more dangerous territory now. I believe it's time to hire armed professionals. Hunting Damon Parkfield was relatively innocuous since anyone in their right mind would expect you to be after him. Opening a larger can of worms as we start researching other women and their possible involvement raises the bar to a whole new level.

"As soon as the ringleaders of this operation catch wind of our intentions, things could get ugly." Jerard paused. "Please be as prudent as possible now. We don't want anyone to figure out what we're doing until absolutely necessary. Take a few months to do the legwork. Track down as many people as you can on paper first. Then we'll reconvene and stake a hit on several all at once. The second anyone realizes our intentions, there's a chance it will get more difficult to prove anything.

"These drugs don't stay in the body very long. Within a few days they're untraceable. We were lucky anything was detected in Ashley. The best plan is to try and corner several possible victims at once, catching them all unaware and running blood samples quickly."

"You have a point, sir."

"Okay, then we're in agreement." Jerard stood and reached out a hand to shake Evan's. "I'll send the files I have on several people by FedEx. You get back home to your mate." He smiled warmly. "Congratulations. I wish you the best."

"Thank you, sir." Evan's chair scraped across the floor as he pushed it aside. A giant weight lifted from his chest.

"We'll be in touch. Use my private line if you need to contact me and keep me updated every few days."

"Will do."

∼

"I'm home." Evan dropped his overnight bag and his briefcase by the front door and took large steps through the living room.

"In here," Ashley called from down the hall.

What was she doing that she didn't race out to greet him? That was so unlike her.

He heard female voices as he headed down the hall and stopped at her studio. He leaned against the door jamb and took in the scene. Ashley stood at the easel. She peered around at him and waved, but her paint brush was poised in the air. Various colors dotted her face and paint shirt.

He loved when she worked. It was the most carefree he ever saw her. If she kept up the pace she'd had lately she would be able to open her own gallery before long. He might be biased, but he thought her work was amazing.

"Give me a second," she said, her gaze returning to the canvas he couldn't see.

"My cue to leave." Samantha stood from the stool she'd been sitting on behind Ashley. "I have a case I need to finish up."

Evan walked her to the door. "Thank you so much for coming over."

Samantha touched his cheek. "Any time, you know that. Ashley and I are getting to be close friends. Anything I can do to help I'm there."

It was Saturday. Luckily Samantha had been able to come over and spend the day with Ashley until Evan could get back. He owed her family a huge debt of gratitude for everything they did for him.

His own parents were much older and lived so far away he only saw them when he made a point of it. Since they'd moved to Florida four years ago to retire, he'd seen them only about once a year. He needed to visit them soon. They were chomping at the bit over the fact that he'd mated and not brought Ashley to see them. It wasn't as though Ashley easily fought crowds and could jump on a plane and go vacationing. And Evan hadn't gone into all the details about Ashley's life with his parents yet. His mother would freak and worry herself sick.

Evan made his way back to Ashley's studio after he saw Samantha out and set the alarm.

She was dipping her brush in a jar of water as he entered. "Just finished. Wanna see?"

He stepped farther into the room and kissed her messy forehead, sure to have smeared blue and yellow paint on his face. How did the woman manage to make such a mess of herself when she worked?

He turned toward the canvas and gasped. "Ash, that's fantastic." A park scene on a sunny day. A child ran through the grass, his little head tipped back to watch the kite streaming behind him. His parents sat on a bench nearby, his father's arm around his mother as they watched with obvious love and admiration.

It was so alive, colorful, perfect.

"Do you like it?" She nibbled on her lower lip when he turned toward her.

He wrapped her in his arms and pulled her in close even though he knew his clothes would be ruined. "Love it. It's so expressive. It seems like the child is actually moving through the scene."

"You have to say that." She slapped his chest with one hand. "But I'm glad you like it."

He backed her up until her ass hit the edge of the desk. "It seems to me I promised to paint you one of these days."

"Ah, that's too bad. I don't have any free canvases available right now." She giggled.

"I never intended to use a canvas." He leaned in to take her mouth in a thorough kiss that past experience told him would leave her mind spinning. When her eyes glazed over, he knew she would be putty in his hands.

Hardly breaking the kiss for one second, he pulled her smock over her head and dropped it on the floor. Next he tugged her T-shirt out of her jeans and whipped it away to join the paint shirt.

Each time he settled his lips back on Ashley. She moaned into his mouth. He could taste her need. She was always so quick to bring to the edge. Not that he was any different. His cock ached. It seemed like he'd been gone a week instead of twenty-four hours.

Evan popped the button on her jeans and lowered the zipper. The sooner he got her naked, the sooner he could make a canvas out of her body. She had no idea what ideas stirred in his mind.

Ashley wiggled her hips as he tugged her jeans down and off. Her feet were bare underneath and as soon as she stood in nothing but her matching pink lace panties and bra he held her away from him for a moment. "You're so gorgeous, baby."

Her stomach dipped as he let his gaze wander over her entire frame. "You aren't so bad yourself," she muttered.

He lifted his hands to cup her breasts and then

expertly popped the front clasp and whisked the lace away.

"We never make it to the bedroom," she teased.

"I don't care. Do you?" He lifted one brow and glanced at her face.

Her cheeks were their usual aroused pink. Her eyes were starting to glaze with lust. She shifted on her feet and he knew her pussy would be wet for him. "No." She whispered that one word with some effort.

Evan dipped his fingers under the thin lace of her thong and slowly, deliberately removed the scrap of material until she stood completely bare to him.

"You're always dressed and I'm always naked," she mumbled. She grabbed his T-shirt and pulled it over his head.

When she reached for his fly, he stopped her, wrapping his hand around hers and pulling it up to his chest. "Not ready for that yet. I can't go slow when you let my dick out. It's too hard."

She laughed as his unintentional pun. "Isn't that the idea? And who said anything about going slow?"

He tapped her nose. "I did." He lifted her onto the desk with both hands at her waist. It was a huge surface. The mahogany would be protected from what he had in mind by the glass top covering the wood. "Lie back, baby." He watched as she gingerly lay against the cold surface, flinching as the glass touched her skin.

"What…?"

He set a finger on her lips. "No talking. Just feel." He turned to the paint pallet behind him and grabbed a brush from the jar next to the bright colors.

"You wouldn't."

"Shh," he admonished, trying to arrange his face in a stern look and sure he failed miserably. "I said I was going to paint you."

He dipped the brush in the pink and held it over her navel. With the tip angled straight down, he waited, watching the drop of paint as it collected at the very end of the brush. Ashley flinched.

"Hold still, baby. Don't move."

She did as he said, but she screamed when the drip finally broke off and landed in her belly button. It was so erotic the way it affected her even though she'd known what was coming.

"Lift your arms over your head." He watched her comply with his wishes. Her shaky hands drifted up above her and landed in the spray of her curls where they lay spread against the desk.

Evan dipped his brush into the drop of paint in her navel and painted a spiral out from the center.

Her stomach hollowed as he worked, and her head rocked back and forth. She squirmed, but not enough for him to admonish her yet.

Loving the look of the deep pink against her skin, he reached for more. This time he started under one breast, slowly swirling a circle of rose around the entire globe, working his way painstakingly toward her nipple.

"Evan…" She gasped as he teased the areola, not quite touching the tip. Instead of giving her any satisfaction there, he gathered more of the acrylic and switched to the other breast. Even without touching the gorgeous tips, they stood more erect than he'd ever seen them. She was the sexiest creature alive.

Her arousal filled the room, her scent making him breathe through his mouth to avoid coming in his pants. He could still taste her on his tongue, but it wasn't as intense. He licked his lips, drawing in the remainder of her flavor from their kiss.

Finally he flicked the soft bristles directly over her nipple. Ashley screeched and bucked her chest. He repeated the action on the other side and then switched back and forth, coating both nipples until all he could see was dark pink paint, made deeper by the rosy color of her areolas underneath. The tips stood tight and firm. He wanted to suck them into his mouth, but not now. Now was for creating his masterpiece.

"Spread your legs, Ash." He dragged the brush in gentle stroked down her thigh as he spoke. "Open for me, baby. I bet this pink will look lovely next to your pussy."

Ashley moaned. Her knees shook as she parted them. The desk wasn't long enough to accommodate her entire body, so her feet remained settled against the glass only a few inches from her center. When she splayed her legs, she opened like a butterfly to his gaze.

She was already so wet, he could see her moisture running down toward her rear hole. Had she ever been taken there? He hoped not. He wanted that tight bud for himself. If it was a trigger for her, he would never force the issue, but he prayed she hadn't been violated in that way. Later. This sexual escapade of theirs was just beginning. They had their whole lives to experience everything they could.

Evan painted a stripe down the inside of both thighs, watching her flinch with each stroke of the brush. He loved the way she remained as still as she did. Even though she thrashed about, her movement was marginal and expected.

He painted the dip behind her knees next, making her lift and lower the butterfly wings of her legs. "Ah ah ah. Stay still. Your canvases don't move around while you work, do they?"

He chuckled and took a moment to watch her face. He adjusted his cock and tried to ignore the demands it screamed in aggravation. The fellow could wait. He was busy.

Another dip into the pink paint and Evan traced a half moon around her pussy on her thighs. He didn't dip too close, knowing she would come the instant he touched her clit. He wanted her to writhe first.

"Evan... God..."

He grinned and painted her outer lips, tiny strokes, just the tip of the brush barely touching her skin. Her pussy grew a deeper pink by itself from the blood that rushed to the surface. He didn't need more paint. The brush strokes alone drove her crazy.

With one hand, he peeled her outer petals apart until he could see her glistening entrance. She panted heavily as he stroked his brush against the sides of her channel. And then he released her.

She heaved for air. "Evan, please..."

"What, baby?" He reached for more paint.

"I need to come so bad. Please."

"Soon. Not yet. I'm not done."

She groaned, her head flopping to one side. Her fingers were balled into tight fists above her head. It was a wonder she was able to hold this position.

Evan let the next drip of paint hover over the hood of her clit. She wasn't looking this time so when the tiny splash finally made contact, she bucked her hips and gasped. "Evan," she screamed.

He set a hand on her lower belly to steady her back against the desk and then circled the paint around her nub as the little tip emerged from the hood all by itself, engorged beyond the norm.

It seemed to pulse in front of him and the dark tip of it actually bobbed as he teased her to within a millimeter of direct contact, his expert strokes circling the tiny nub of need mercilessly.

Finally, he put her out of her misery, brushing firmly right against her clit.

She moaned and squirmed, but he held the brush directly on the sensitive center of her arousal. He released her belly with his other hand and switched the hand holding the brush so he could drag his fingers through her wet folds.

She stiffened immediately, her legs rigid in their splayed position, her ass lifted off the desk. The second he pushed two fingers into her she shattered. Her entire body participated in the orgasm, shaking and convulsing as though much more than her pussy were involved.

As the tremors subsided, her hands flew down and

pushed the brush from her clit. "Too much," she mumbled.

Evan set the brush aside and eased his fingers from inside her, continuing to sooth her skin as she regained her breath. "That was amazing," he said. "Thank you."

She chuckled, deeper than her usual laugh. "Thank me?"

"Yep, I'll never tire of watching you come. It humbles me."

"It makes me crave your cock when you do that. It feels so good, but it isn't enough." She squirmed around to see him better. "Why are you still wearing your jeans?"

He released her folds, kicked off his shoes, and shrugged his pants off, and then lowered his underwear to the ground. "What jeans?" He leaned down to tug off his socks and then stood completely bared to her gaze.

"How do you stay so tight and firm?" she asked and she pulled her languid body upright. She wasn't looking at his crotch. Her gaze wandered his shoulders and chest.

He didn't point out her mixed message. "I work out."

"When? I never see you."

"I've been to every gym in the country while traveling." He grinned as he took her into his embrace, her legs straddling him as she scooted to the edge of the desk. "And I run." He let his gaze land on hers.

"I haven't seen you run."

"I don't do it very often in human form." He brushed her hair from her face. "I have a quiet spot I like to go to and shift," he added, watching her reaction.

"Oh, right. That." She bit her lip and tried to kiss him, but he held her back.

"Soon, Ash. I want you to run free with me."

She nodded. "Soon." She wouldn't make eye contact this time. She still insisted she wasn't ready. He knew she felt very safe when she was with him, so he doubted her reluctance had as much to do with Damon still being on the loose as with her fear that after so many years she wouldn't be able to shift.

It was rare for a wolf to go so long without shifting, but it wasn't unheard of. And she was young. He knew if he got her over her mental hurdles, she'd be fine. It would be so freeing for her to shift and let herself go.

But, that was for later. Right now he needed to be inside her. And without another word, he pushed himself into her warmth.

She squeezed him to her as though she needed the most contact she could get with his body. He understood completely.

The desk was the right height for him to stand and take her. He held her thighs as he pushed into her again and again, keeping her from scooting back against the slick surface.

"Look at us." He angled his gaze down to where they connected. Paint smeared both of their chests and thighs.

"That's hot." She reached between them and stroked her clit while he held on to her. She'd never been that bold before, and he was glad to see her blossoming and taking the initiative to ensure she got what she needed.

"Does that feel good, baby?"

"So good..." She tipped her head back, making her chest arch. She was a vision with her swan neck extended and her dainty fingers stroking herself perfectly. "Harder," she demanded.

Evan closed his eyes and concentrated on her wishes. He increased the pace and luxuriated in her tightness. It was hard to hold on. They were both so slippery.

Ashley scooted forward several times. Finally she went stiff and he opened his eyes to find her pinching her clit between her fingers. Every time she came, it pushed him over the edge. He couldn't swallow past the love he felt for her as his orgasm swept through him, forcing itself against the end of her passage.

She released her clit and ran her hands up his painted chest, smearing the pink over his shoulders and down his back. "Pink is good on you." She giggled as he caught his breath.

He didn't want to pull out of her. If he could, he'd stay inside her warmth forever.

But the reality was, they were a mess.

In order to cut down on the cleanup, he heaved her off the desk. "Wrap your legs around me and hold on." Still embedded inside her, he padded down the hall, into the master bedroom, and straight for the bath. He flipped on the shower with one hand and leaned her back against the shower door while he waited for the water to heat.

He gazed into her eyes, deep green pools of love. Before he opened the shower and lost the moment, he nuzzled her neck and inhaled the scent of their lovemaking mixed with the distinct smell of acrylics. He never wanted to forget this moment.

~

Damon slammed the last of his things into his bag and looked around the ragged hellhole he'd been living in for the last week. His life was a wreck. Ruined by whoever ran the fucking Romulus.

He'd given up on them and their promises. Perhaps they would be glad for him to go rogue so they didn't have to bother with him anymore.

Were there others like him out there? Other shifters in the same predicament who'd fallen for the empty promises of home, hearth, and happiness from these bastards?

He may never know, but at this point he was too tired to continue to care.

He was going it alone. He'd already smashed the cell phone and thrown the pieces into the toilet. The phone number to the Romulus would forever be burned into his head, but those fuckers had no way to get ahold of him.

Damon had no idea what he would do first, but he had every intention of finding a giant vacant stretch of wooded land in the Midwest somewhere and spending a great deal of time in wolf form. Hell, maybe forever. He could shift and reclaim his life as a wolf. It would be easier than trying to find work and sustain himself in human form.

He shook his head as he heaved his duffle off the

bed. Nope. That would be too easy. Besides, he had a grudge to avenge. No matter what else had happened and under what pretenses, that bitch Ashley started all his problems with her unwillingness to comply as a good mate should.

Who the fuck did she think she was denying she was his mate and torturing him with her whining for all those years? She should have known her place, drugs or no drugs, Romulus or not. Neither of those factors should have played a role in her job as his mate.

She'd failed him. And she would pay.

As soon as he could get his feet under him and gather his wits, he would find that bitch and make her sorry she'd ever left him...

CHAPTER 21

Two months later...

Ashley stood at the doorway to Evan's office, watching him work. She leaned against the frame and crossed her legs. She thought the smell of coffee wafting up from the mug in her hands would lure him to look up, but he was so intent on his research he didn't budge.

His shoulders must hurt from sitting like that for so long, peering over documents or staring into the computer.

She was on break between classes and planning to take a full load the next semester. She intended to take several classes at the local campus, if she could build up the nerve. Her counselor was impressed with her progress. She'd even gone so far as to tell Ashley she hadn't seen anyone in her sort of predicament come around so fast.

Ashley knew she owed every step toward freedom to Evan.

She cleared her throat and waited. Finally he glanced up. A smile spread across his face, erasing the furrow in his brow. "Hi, baby." He motioned her forward. When she reached his side and handed him the mug, he pulled her into his lap. "I'm sorry I've been so reoccupied lately."

"Are you close? Have you found more of the women?" She knew a little about his work, not everything, but enough to grasp the seriousness of the job.

"Eleven so far. We are hoping for a few more before we move in."

"And by 'we' you mean…?"

"The hired professionals. Not me." He kissed her lips. "Ready to go?"

She narrowed her gaze at him. "I suppose, but it would be nice if you told me where we're going." Surprises weren't her favorite and he'd given her very few details about his plans for today. The most she'd gotten from him was it didn't matter what she wore and they'd be taking the car. That wasn't much.

"It wouldn't be a surprise if I told you, would it?" He stood, depositing her on the ground and taking her hand. He grabbed the coffee with his free hand and tugged her from the room.

She moved a bit reluctantly, somewhat uneasy about his plans. This was unlike him. He'd never planned a secret outing and left her guessing.

Evan wandered into the kitchen and deposited his half-empty coffee mug on the counter.

Ashley narrowed her gaze at him. "I'm not sure I'm going to like this."

"Only one way to find out." He smirked and nodded toward the door. "Let's go."

"How long will we be gone? Do I need a jacket?"

"Stop asking questions. You aren't going to get anything else out of me." He winked at her as he opened the front door.

She followed and soon they were driving down the highway. She watched the scenery as they moved away from the house and the business of the suburbs.

She swallowed hard when he pulled off the highway and down a back road. "Evan…"

He grasped her hand and squeezed, but said nothing. When he finally pulled over on the side of the road and turned off the car, there was no longer any doubt about what he had in mind. He swiveled his body to face her, not releasing her hand. His smile was forced. "Do this for me, baby. I'm only asking you to try."

She licked her lips. "I'm not even sure if I can. You know that."

"And what's the harm in giving it a shot?"

She glanced down at her lap, her hands trembling. She yanked her hand from his grasp. *What if I can't shift?* She didn't want to face that eventuality.

"I'll be right by your side. We have never seen or heard from Parkfield in months. You know the chances that he followed us out here are nil. There's nothing to be afraid of."

"That's not even my fear any more, Evan. I'm far more scared of failure."

He reached for her shoulder with one hand and tipped her chin up with the other. "You won't fail. I just know it. And the longer you wait to shift, the harder it will be. This is important to me. I want us to be able to run free together. I want our kids to be able to run with us someday. Don't let your fear rule you."

She took a deep breath. It meant so much to him. And to be honest, she'd been itching to shift for months. It was very unusual for a shifter to go five years without taking their wolf form. And it wasn't unheard of for shifters to lose touch with that part of themselves over the passage of time. Some ended up blending in with the general human population, their abilities forgotten and lost over generations.

"I want this. I do."

"Then let's do it."

Ashley climbed out of the car and circled around to the driver's side. She leaned her butt against the back door and set her hands on her knees.

Evan rubbed her back. "Relax. If you can't pull it off this time, we'll try again. No pressure. Just an attempt."

With a fortifying deep breath, she righted herself. "I'm ready." She didn't feel as ready as her voice proclaimed, but she hoped the words alone would help her prepare.

Evan slowly stripped his clothes and set them on the front seat. "My favorite part about shifting is the thought that someone could come along, find my car, and think I got taken in the Rapture." He then reached under the steering wheel and placed his shoes on the floorboard. "I like to add this little part to make their eyes bug out." He laughed and Ashley couldn't help giggling at his attempt to calm her.

"That's evil."

"Yeah well, I seriously hope to impress some Christians someday with my purity."

Ashley let her gaze roam up Evan's body from his feet to his face as he turned toward her. She licked her lips.

"Don't look at me like that." He playfully covered her eyes. "We're here to run, remember?" His lips landed on her ear and she shivered as he whispered the words, his warm breath tickling her earlobe.

Instead of waiting for her, he took the liberty of undressing her himself, pulling her shirt over her head and tossing it into the car.

"Will they think we were both sitting in the driver's seat?" she teased as she removed her own pants. "Think of the shock when someone finds that arrangement." She tossed her jeans onto the pile. "In fact, I'm feeling devious enough to add to your game. Why don't you arrange my clothes so it appears we were fucking in the parked car when the apocalypse occurred?"

He plucked her bra from her fingers as she slipped it down her arms. "Let's not get carried away. Someone might have a heart attack." He grinned at her as she removed the last of her clothing. "Ready?"

"I guess." She shivered, even though the air was warm. It was early June in the Midwest and already summer was descending.

"You want me to shift first? Or stay in human form and wait for you?"

"No. Go ahead. Maybe I'll derive inspiration from your change." *I hope.*

Ashley took a step back and watched as Evan shut the car door and stowed the key under the rim of the front tire. "It's not the best-laid plan, but hey, I figure if someone comes upon my car and waits for me scratching their head, I'm going to have way bigger problems explaining my nudity than the fact that they could have stolen the vehicle."

Ashley bit her lip. He was rambling. He might have been as nervous as she was. The idea endeared her. She smiled when he cracked his neck and stretched his shoulders as though a few bone pops would help the transition. She knew he was stalling. Giving her time to adjust.

She raised her eyebrows when he glanced at her.

"Okay, I'm shifting." It took him seconds to alter forms. One moment he was smiling at her and the next he dropped onto all fours, bones popping, face lengthening, fur elongating.

She'd shifted many times as a teen, but she hadn't recalled the simplicity of the task. Now she really worried she didn't have it in her.

Evan sauntered up to her side and rubbed his head against her leg. His eyes were the same deep brown in wolf form as human, his fur a dark wavy mass she wanted to sink her hands into. And she did. She knelt at his side and pulled him against her, wrapping her arms around his neck. She inhaled his scent and recognized it as distinctly Evan. She'd know him anywhere in any form.

Squatting beside him, still stroking his lean neck, she closed her eyes and used his massive size to link her to the other world she wanted to cross into. She tipped her head back toward the sky and breathed deeply of the mixed scent of the clean forest air and Evan.

Seconds ticked by. Evan stayed still at her side, letting her squeeze his fur in her palm. She calmed with each breath, centering herself with nature.

When she tilted her face back down and met his warm gaze, a tingling started in her arms and worked through her body. She stiffened against the strange sensation before her memory flooded to the surface and she recalled the natural steps of undergoing the transformation years before.

Concentrating on her wolf form, she visualized herself dashing through the trees at a speed she could never accomplish as a human. The wind would whip her fur away from her face and all her senses would heighten to allow her to easily avoid obstacles and move at incredible speeds.

She grew anxious to know that feeling again. Now. With Evan at her side, the experience would have new meaning. She knew she could do this.

She blinked as another wave of the tingling caressed her skin, this time less shocking than the first. It increased in intensity and she let it ride forward as though on an ocean wave. Instead of fighting it in fear, she let herself float that wave higher and higher…until at last her body did what it was born to do. The last part was the easy part. As soon as she tuned her mind into the right channel, she easily shifted as fast as Evan had.

She stood before him and blinked. She lifted a paw and patted at him. Her fur was several shades lighter than his and a mixture of browns and blondes that closely resembled her human hair.

Evan seemed to grin at her, if wolves could do such a thing. He nuzzled her neck against his and then nodded behind him. It was time to run.

Ashley was beyond ready now. She was eager. Anxious. Her steps faltered for only a few steps before she got her wolf paws under her and took off behind her mate. It was like riding a bike. The coordination took only moments to come back to her and soon she was trotting behind her mate in a mad dash for the tree line.

Well, at first it seemed quick at least. But soon she wanted more, craved the speed and realized he was keeping his pace slow to allow her time to acclimate. She didn't need more time. She needed speed.

She rushed past him and took the lead, enjoying the freedom and silently thanking God she'd met a man who was perfect in so many ways…including luring her out and forcing her to face her other half. He was a gem and she would never take him for granted.

CHAPTER 22

Evan wrapped his body around his mate and held her back against his front. He nuzzled his face into her neck and nibbled a path to her ear. It was still early, but he needed to get up soon. "I have to go into the office today," he murmured against her ear, knowing he was tickling her with his breath. He loved the way she squirmed to get out of the path of his tongue, but he was too big for her to battle.

He'd intentionally waited until now to tell her he was leaving for the day. She slept better without the worry of his absence. And she'd slept sound and hard after he'd worn her out with their run.

This time he'd planned in advance. Samantha was off today and she'd agreed to come over and spend the day with Ashley. It would make Ashley calmer and keep Evan from worrying about her during meetings.

"Mmm." She snuggled into his body as though she could get closer and lessen the distance between them. Her fine tush wiggled against his cock.

Evan brought one hand down and splayed it against her belly to still her. She didn't have to ask. He had every intention of making love to her before he left the house, but preferably not so fast he couldn't enjoy it, drag it out. "Hold still, imp."

He could cover her entire torso with the one hand and he inched it up until he cupped a breast in his palm. Her breathing hitched as he gently stroked the tender skin of the underside of her soft globe. When she arched into his hand, he brushed his thumb over her nipple until it stood at attention.

Ashley moaned and gripped his forearm with both hands. "Evan..." His name, whispered on a breath, dragged out for several seconds. He adored the way she called to him when she was needy.

Evan teased both nipples, alternately switching back and forth to caress them with the barest touch.

When Ashley moaned and her legs started squirming under the one he'd pinned her with, he smoothed a line down her belly and danced his fingers around her clit.

"Evan..." she repeated, wiggling her ass once again against his rock-hard cock.

Evan bucked his hips back to keep her from touching him. He entwined her top leg with his and dragged the limb back, opening her up to his touch. The scent of her arousal filled the room as the blankets got tugged away, twisted around his leg.

"Oh, baby. So horny already." He inhaled long and slow, loving the smell of her as she filled his lungs.

He lowered his hand farther to drag one finger

through her folds. Wetness covered his digit. He spread her moisture up toward her clit and flicked his finger over the distended nub.

Ashley squirmed but Evan anticipated her movement. He gripped her firmly across her waist with the arm underneath her and kissed her neck. "So hot, baby." He stroked back through her folds and then pushed two fingers inside her, curving them toward her belly. Her G-spot was so sensitive to his touch. Anytime he brushed the ball of nerves inside her opening, she stilled.

He couldn't see her eyes with her face angled away from him, but he knew they would be rolled back. She always lost herself to focus on the impending orgasm when he had her in this position. It was powerful and his dick ached with want.

Sharp pants escaped her lips as she braced herself against his touch. Her fingers gripped his arm firmer, her nails digging into his skin. She'd leave half-moon marks, but he didn't care. He'd wear them with pride.

"Come for me, baby," he urged. As he spoke, he pressed his thumb into her clit and flicked his fingers rapidly over her G-spot.

Ashley shattered around him, her entire body pulsing as she milked his fingers and shuddered from head to toe. "Evan!" She screamed his name that time, a sharp burst of sound that echoed in the room.

As her body came down from its high, he continued to stroke her, both inside and out. He knew she'd need more. A low hum escaped her lips as she climbed back to the top. "I need you. Please, stop teasing." She wiggled in his arms, her ass reaching back to entice him.

He needed no such encouragement. In the blink of an eye he had her on her back and lined his cock up with her swollen pussy. He stroked through her folds, back and forth, tempting her with the tip of his dick.

"Now, Evan."

He chuckled at her demand. God, he loved this woman. In one thrust, he pressed into her tightness, his knees settling between her legs to push them open farther.

He had to hold himself steady when he was fully seated in order to get a grip and keep from coming too fast. He fit inside her so perfectly and her body seemed to hug his cock, drawing it deeper with each breath.

Evan slowly pulled out and reentered her warmth. He gritted his teeth to stave off his orgasm as she lifted her ass to meet every stroke.

Evan grabbed both her hands, twined his fingers with hers, and lifted them high above her head as he picked up the pace. He needed her to come again and knew the pressure of his body would do the trick before he released himself into her.

Tiny incoherent sounds escaped Ashley's mouth with each thrust. He nudged her hair out of her face with his chin and nibbled her neck until he reached her mouth. "I love you." And then he kissed her. His deep and thorough invasion of her mouth filled all his senses, overwhelming him with the impact she had on him. She owned him. It wasn't the other way around at all. Until the day he died, she would be the ruler of his universe.

When Ashley's body tightened beneath him, Evan couldn't hold off any longer. He pressed into her fully and held his breath as he filled her with his seed.

Ashley shivered as her orgasm subsided. Her body lay limp against the sheets, and Evan collapsed along one side of her, careful not to crush her but not wanting to lose contact with her skin.

They lay panting for several moments before Evan had the energy to sweep Ashley's blonde locks away from her face and kiss her once again. "I have to get up."

She smiled. "Are you sure? You mentioned that a bit ago and I still have you with me."

He pinched her side playfully, making her squirm. "You're the death of me. A horrible influence." He pulled himself reluctantly from her body, caressing her belly with the tips of his fingers as he sat. "Samantha is coming over this morning. Girl time."

"Right." Ashley turned to her side and watched him climb from the bed. "You don't have to keep protecting my sensitive feelings, you know. It's a fact I don't like to be alone. I love you for asking her to come over. You can tell it like it is." She smiled and he wanted nothing more than to climb back into the warm bed with her and make love until they both couldn't walk.

Instead, he closed his eyes against her alluring coy grin and backed into the adjoining bathroom. A shower would work wonders toward the transition between his sexy mate and their warm bed and his cold hard office.

Sure, if you believe that, I'll sell you some oranges grown in Greenland.

~

Ten minutes after Evan left, Ashley watched Samantha pull into the driveway and dash toward the house.

"So sorry," she blurted as she let herself in and reset the alarm. "I wanted to be here before Evan left." Samantha had all the alarm codes memorized and Ashley was grateful for the woman's precision when it came to safety.

Ashley stepped from the kitchen, two warm mugs in hand. She knew Samantha would need the steaming elixir first thing when she came through the door. "Coffee?"

"Bless you." She took a sip and her eyes rolled back as she wiggled out of her coat and tossed it across the back of the couch. She plopped down on one cushion and tipped her head back. "So, what do you want to do today?"

Ashley laughed. "Like you don't have a briefcase full of work with you." She nodded toward the small leather case Samantha had dropped at the door. The woman was a workhorse. She would have at least six cases pending she needed to research. "Besides, I'm in the middle of a project." She lifted her nose as though she had the right to be snotty because her painting was so über important. And then she giggled again.

"Awesome. What are you working on? Can I see?"

"Not yet." Ashley hated sharing her work midway through. She didn't like to see the strange scrutiny on anyone's face as they tried to decipher where she was going with a particular project. It tamped down on her muse.

"I'm so glad you're painting again."

"It relaxes me. I don't care if I never sell a piece as long as it calms me."

"Oh, you will, girl. It's fantastic. One of these days we'll be lined up to see your work in a famous art show."

"Whatever." Ashley rolled her eyes. "But I'm going to get to work while I'm feeling it. You need anything?" Sure, Samantha had come over and the woman was pretending they were supposed to sit around giggling and chatting all day, but Ashley knew better. Samantha never lacked for work. She needed to get out of the woman's way, be grateful for the friendship that brought her here, and head for her studio.

Samantha stood. "Nope. I'll just spread out on your dining room table if you insist and plow through a few depositions."

"Sounds…awful." Ashley scrunched up her face as she backed out of the room. "I'll be much happier in a smock with paint splattered all around me."

She left her friend and padded down the hall. Ashley stood at the entrance to her studio, admiring her mess, so blessed to have everything a woman could possibly want right at her fingertips.

CHAPTER 23

Damon set his binoculars in his lap and chuckled to himself. Stupid women. How on earth did that asshole, Evan, think he could protect Ashley with another woman? They were weak creatures, all of them. This would be too easy.

It was all planned. Damon had only been waiting for the perfect opportunity to swoop in and take Ashley. She was useless to him. Disobedient and sterile. But he wouldn't stand for her thinking she'd outsmarted him in the end. The bitch would pay. First he'd kidnap her from her mock-safe environment and then he'd toy with her for days before he killed her, painfully. He was completely rogue now. It didn't matter if he added murder to his repertoire.

Weeks he'd waited for this day.

He left his car two doors down and got out. In moments he approached Evan's home from the side. Before either woman inside knew what was happening, he kicked the back door in and stepped into the kitchen.

Some friend of Ashley's was at the sink and she screamed when the alarm sounded, dropping the mug she was holding on the tile and shattering it into a million pieces. It must have been empty because there was no splash of scalding coffee. Shame. He'd have been more gratified if she'd gotten burned.

Damon had his arm around her neck and dragged her to the alarm panel before she could get away. "Turn it off," he commanded. He didn't care that the police had already been informed. He didn't intend to be there long enough for it to matter. Let them come. He'd be long gone by then.

The woman reached with a trembling finger and typed in four numbers. He was sure they were a distress call, but it didn't matter as long as he moved fast and didn't have to listen to that blaring noise any longer.

In the renewed silence, Damon dragged the woman down the hall.

A loud clatter inside the first door on the left told him where Ashley was located. Sure enough, when he kicked the door open with his foot, he found her scrambling away from an overturned easel. She sat on her ass amidst splattering paint, blue and green drops dripping from her hair. "Leave Samantha out of this, Damon." She scuffed her tennis shoes across the floor, trying to get purchase. Finally she pulled herself upright and flattened herself against the wall. "She has nothing to do with us, Damon." Her voice shook as she spoke.

Damon chuckled. "Really? That's so sweet, Ash. But I think her presence is perfect for what I have in mind. Samantha, is it? What a nice name." He squeezed her tighter, knowing he was cutting off her airway. Her feet barely reached the ground in front of him and she held on to his forearm with both hands to keep from choking. Wheezing breaths were all he heard from her. Good. He didn't have to listen to the bitch whine.

"What do you want, Damon?" Ashley's face turned white. Her eyes remained glued to her friend.

"Look at me, bitch."

She jerked her gaze to his.

"Here's how this is going to work." He held Samantha with one arm and pulled a knife from the sheath on his belt with the other. God how he loved the fear he saw in Ashley's face, her eyes wide, her mouth open. He almost wished she would scream. Instead she swallowed around her fear and stared at him in disbelief. He watched her long lean throat working.

Damon lifted the knife to Samantha's throat. He nicked her neck with the serrated edges, intentionally increasing the fear in Ashley's eyes. When he glanced at Samantha, he found her neck bleeding in several places and almost kissed the bone handle of his favorite hunting knife. "You come with me nicely and I'll let the bitch live. You put up a fight and I'll kill her in an instant. Which is it?"

Ashley shuffled forward two steps. "Let her go, Damon."

Damon squeezed harder, glancing at Samantha's face and noting how long she could go like this before she passed out.

He tugged her forward, enjoying seeing the life ebb out of her face.

"Fine. Damon. Put her down. I'll go with you." Ashley's voice creaked as she spoke. He narrowed his gaze. It didn't matter to him whether Samantha lived or died today, as long as he took Ashley with him alive.

"You're my mate. What made you think you could fuck another man?" *Don't let your emotions get in the way of this task, Damon.*

"I… I'm sorry, Damon. You're right. I was… confused. I shouldn't have left you." Ashley inched toward him.

Perfect. In a minute she'd be close enough for him to drop Samantha and grab Ashley. In two minutes he'd have her hogtied, run and get the car, pull it in the garage, and stuff her in the trunk. If she suffocated in there, so be it.

His fingers grew stiff from holding the knife and he flexed them individually to release the tension. His other arm strained in the stronghold he had around Samantha's neck.

Suddenly Ashley tripped over the easel and fell forward into a gallon of white paint sitting on a stool. The paint went flying and slashed all over Samantha and Damon. He fumed, narrowing his gaze at her. "You did that on purpose."

~

Ashley could only pray her actions would prove helpful in some way. She was desperate. Slippery paint couldn't hurt the situation. She'd hoped the paint would slosh up higher than it had and cause Damon to release Samantha. Unfortunately, it hadn't.

What she needed was time. She knew the police had been notified and were on their way. They would have called Evan too. But how long would it take? How long could she stall?

Ashley took a step back. "I'm so sorry. I didn't realize I'd left the lid off that paint."

Damon looked around. "You're painting again."

"Yes," Ashley muttered. She didn't want to antagonize him any more than necessary. She had no idea how he might react to her work. He hadn't permitted her to paint often while she'd been under his thumb. He'd used it as a reward for good behavior.

Samantha picked that moment while Damon was distracted to kick him hard in the shin. It had to be difficult since her entire body was supported by his grip on her neck.

"You bitch," he bellowed. When he twisted to get a better grip, he stepped in the paint and slipped.

Ashley watched as though in slow motion as both of them went down. Damon, unwilling to let go of his victim, skidded across the floor until he couldn't keep his balance. He released Samantha with a shove, pushing her toward the far wall. But Samantha couldn't get purchase either on the thick paint and she flailed her arms to keep from losing traction when her feet hit the ground. Her face was pale, almost blue, and the lack of oxygen didn't help.

In horror, Ashley reached out too late to keep

Samantha from slamming head first into the ground. She hit with a loud thump and went completely limp.

Oh my God! Ashley stared at her brother's mate, panic setting in. Was she dead? She couldn't tell if her chest was rising and falling or not. Samantha didn't move a muscle. So still.

Ashley dashed toward Samantha, determined to help save her friend...her family...her sister-in-law. But before she could reach her, Damon grabbed her by the leg and pulled her down hard. She hit the floor chin first, her jaw slamming shut and her teeth clanking together. Her entire head exploded with pain and she screamed louder than she'd ever screamed in her life.

If she let him take her, she'd never see Evan again. She'd never live to see tomorrow. No. She either had to get away or die trying. She would not be taken alive by this bastard to be tortured yet again.

Damon pulled her ankle, dragging her toward him until he held her thigh. She couldn't get purchase on anything on the floor. Her hands were slick with paint, her entire body now covered in the white mess. Even her face was splattered from hitting the floor.

Her head swam, her vision clouded from the impact. She squirmed to get away, but he was stronger. She kicked at him, hitting his face hard with her shoe, but that only made him angrier.

"Stop fighting me, bitch. You're half my size. You won't win. You're mine and you'll do as I say or suffer the repercussions."

Repercussion? Like being tortured, raped, and locked up for days on end? No, thanks.

Ashley kicked harder, trying to free her leg. She found herself being dragged across the floor and she flattened her palms on the hardwood in an effort to gain some sort of traction.

Nothing. There was nothing to grab onto. Panic. Fear seized her and she shook her head to clear the fog. Her vision still blurry, she couldn't get her bearings straight.

She got caught up on the legs of the easel that had collapsed before he'd entered the room. She'd tripped over it when the alarm had sounded and it had crashed with a loud bang.

Shit. Ashley flailed her arms around her, sweeping them across the floor. Maybe she could grab a leg of the easel and swing it around to hit him.

She found the end of one leg, but it wouldn't budge. It was still attached to the frame. Useless.

And then her other hand swiped at something under the paint. Something cold and firm...and sharp. *The knife.* He must have dropped it when he slipped and fell.

She wrapped her hand around the handle, thankful she hadn't cut herself. She knew it was sharp. It had snagged Samantha's skin in several places.

Now she prayed she'd have the opportunity to use it before Damon realized she had it.

Damon continued to tow her in and she squealed and kept striving for something to hold on to with her free hand. Until she had the right moment, she would keep her treasure to herself.

"You're only making things worse for yourself, Ash. This flailing isn't helping your case. Your friend is already dead. You're next. You want this to go the hard way or the easy way?"

Was there an easy way to die? Hell, if she had to, she'd stab herself in the chest before she'd leave with him.

Ashley had an idea. She stopped fighting and relaxed her legs, hoping he would loosen his grip.

"Ah, so finally you come to your senses, bitch." He let go and stood carefully amidst the paint. "Why do you need so damn much paint for canvases?" He glanced around the room, wiping paint from his hands onto his equally sticky pants.

Good. Conversation. She could do this. Buy more time. "It covers the canvas before I start to work." *Stupid asshole*. Still on her belly, she twisted her face around to see him. Judge his state of mind.

He whipped his gaze toward her and narrowed his eyes. "Get up."

Not a chance in hell.

"Now, bitch. You've caused me enough trouble for one day. We're getting out of here before your fuck buddy returns."

She flinched at the terminology but didn't let her face change. Instead she carefully turned over onto her back. She had to release the knife at her side to do so, but she quickly found it with her other hand, her dominant hand.

She gripped the handle once again and stared up at the face of a demon. He reached for her. "I said, get up," he shouted.

Come to me instead, you bastard.

She didn't move. If he wanted her, he was going to have to come and get her. And she could only hope she would be able to stab him and do enough damage to get away. If only she could get out of the house. She could scream for help. Surely someone would hear her.

Damon stepped between her legs. The moment he leaned forward to grab her himself, she whipped one leg out, causing him to fall forward. In a flash, he was crashing toward her. She only had a second, but that's all she needed.

Ashley yanked the long serrated blade up in front of her, the tip pointing straight out.

Damon never saw it coming. He could have done nothing to stop his own demise anyway. It was too late. He fell straight onto the blade, his chest crashing over the knife until it was completely embedded inside him.

His eyes opened wide for an instant, his mouth parted, words that would never be spoken on the tip of his tongue.

Before he completely collapsed on top of her, Ashley scrambled to get out from under him. She heaved at his chest with all her strength to flip him off her. He landed on his back beside her and she kicked away from him, her feet fighting against the slippery mess of paint and blood. The knife remained in her hand though she had no idea how she'd managed to dislodge it. She wasn't willing to let go. What if he jumped back up?

As soon as she was a few feet away she heaved for air, not realizing she'd been holding her breath. She scampered to stand and looked down at Damon's body for a moment. His eyes were open, never to blink again.

A moan caught her attention. Samantha. She whipped her gaze to her friend on the other side of the room and struggled to slide across the floor with as much care as she could to avoid falling.

She knelt beside Samantha and wiped the paint and hair from her face, not wanting to hurt her any more than she already was by moving her. But Samantha surprised her by pulling herself to a sitting position.

"God, Sam. You're okay." Ashley grabbed her friend's arm to assure herself she was indeed alive.

"My head hurts like a motherfucker." She glanced to the side and gasped. "Not as bad as his though." She lifted her gaze back to Ashley and smiled. "You did it. You fucking killed the bastard." Her voice was rough.

Ashley stood and backed up a few paces. "I'll go to jail, won't I?" She shook her head. "I'm a murderer."

"No. Sweetie…you're not a murderer. He is. You won't be responsible for any more than answering a few questions at the scene. He came here to kill you—and me, for that matter. You acted in self-defense. That's different."

"Are you sure?" What if she never got to hold Evan again or feel his arms around her?

"Absolutely."

Ashley shifted her gaze to the dead man on the floor. Blood. So much blood. Who knew the human body held so much blood? It pumped out of his chest where the knife had been and blended with the white paint to create a stream of pink across the floor.

Ashley glanced down at the knife in her hand and suddenly released it as though it had the plague. If she never touched another knife in her life, it would be too soon. It clattered to the floor and she watched as it bounced into the paint.

Sirens. She lifted her gaze and listened. The police were coming. The sirens grew louder by the moment and her chest began to pound. What if Samantha was wrong? What if they arrested her? She'd killed a man. Never mind he was a bad man.

She looked back down at his body, memorizing this scene so she could replay it again in the future. She never wanted to forget his dead lifeless body splayed out on the floor. It would cut down on the nightmares and help her remember she was alive and he could never hurt her again. No matter what Fate lay in front of her.

Ashley closed her eyes as she listened to the squeal of police vehicles screeching to a halt around her house.

She took a deep breath. *It's going to be okay... It has to be.*

EPILOGUE

Evan held his mate close. He wrapped his arms around her from behind and leaned in to breathe her in—a mixture of her shampoo, her girly soaps and her own personal scent.

The warm breeze coming off the ocean whipped around them both, blowing her hair into his face. He didn't care. His vision was blocked to the sunset she'd so badly wanted to see over the endless water. It had been her dream, not his. He didn't care if he never saw another sunset as long as he had her with him.

He'd insisted on a vacation after they'd finally worked through the red tape with the police department. She'd worried endlessly about being arrested and it had taken days to convince her no one was going to accuse her of murder.

When she said she'd wanted to see the ocean, Evan had known immediately they would come to Florida and she could meet his parents. His mother had been ecstatic when Evan told her they were coming. She'd rolled out the red carpet and prepared the guest room as though he and Ashley were royalty.

Ashley and his mom hit it off in minutes, sharing their love of art as Veronica had given Ashley a tour of the entire beach house. Evan's father, Roland, was more reserved, but Evan had seen the twinkle in his father's eye as he'd congratulated the two of them on their mating.

The beach house was the perfect vacation spot. They could enjoy endless sun and warm water, while sleeping soundly in a home protected by Evan's parents. He'd known Ashley would relax better with more people in the home. Eventually they would have their own place, but in the meantime, his little mate relaxed incrementally the more people she had surrounding her.

As much as he wanted her all to himself, he enjoyed her calm and peace more.

Evan still worried about whoever Damon's supplier was. It niggled in the back of his mind that Damon hadn't acted alone. Someone had to have been supplying him with the drug he'd used on Ashley. The evidence concerning other women was piling up. Any day now he knew a team of people were poised to advance and make a sweep in several cities at once.

The only thing that calmed Evan was convincing himself the drug supplier had no motive to be interested in Ashley. She was a victim and no threat to the chain of command.

Ashley had woken up screaming every night for the first several nights, sweat pouring off her body and soaking the sheets where they slept in her childhood room at her parents' house.

They'd never go back to the house he'd owned when he met her again. There were very few things they even wanted to salvage from the place that now held so many bad memories. Josh and Nathan had gone in to retrieve her artwork and several other items of importance. They'd packed up Evan's office and moved everything to Ashley's parents'. The rest would be sold along with the house.

They would build another, design it together as soon as she was up to it.

For now, they were taking a week to rest and recuperate.

He closed his eyes and held her tighter until she squirmed. She giggled. "Evan, you're going to break a rib. Not so tight."

He smiled into her neck and nibbled his way to the back of her ear. So sensitive. Her skin was so smooth. He dragged his tongue down the long muscle.

Ashley squirmed to get away from him. "Stop licking me. It's weird." But her voice was jovial. She wasn't the least bit chagrined by his attention. In fact, he knew from experience how much she liked it when he licked a path across her neck, her nipple, her clit, the soft folds of her pussy…

He stopped anyway and lifted his gaze toward the setting sun.

"It's so beautiful," she muttered under her breath. She twisted her head to briefly look into his eyes. "Thank you."

"For what?" he teased.

"For bringing me here. For loving me. For making me the happiest woman on the planet. I love you." Her face lit up as she said those words. She said them often, but they couldn't be said enough. He would never tire of hearing them from her lips.

He was so lucky to have found her. It would take a long time for her to heal fully, but she was strong. His little mate was made of fire. She would survive and thrive. And it was a good thing because... "Ashley, I need to tell you something." He ran his palms down her torso and splayed them across her belly.

"What?" She turned to him again, worry filling her eyes as they widened.

"You're pregnant."

"What?" She nearly screamed. She twisted in his arms until she faced him, the sunset forgotten. "How do you know?" She shook her head.

"I can smell it, baby." He grinned at her. "And you've been ignoring the signs."

"What signs?" She bit her lip, not willing to accept his words, to hope.

"You've been tired. You've been queasy. You've had trouble eating in the morning. Your breasts are fuller." For emphasis, and because he couldn't resist, he lifted his hands to her chest and lifted the swollen globes in each palm. He set his forehead on her temple as her mouth opened. "And your nipples are sensitive," he added, stroking his thumbs over the distended tips, making her moan.

Her eyes shut. Her chest pounded under his attention. "I thought I was upset from…"

"I know you did. But believe me, you're pregnant. You're going to have a sweet little girl in about seven months that looks like you, and I'm going to wrap her around my finger and spoil her until she's so rotten no man ever wants to take her away."

Ashley giggled and opened her eyes. "You can't know it's a girl."

"Nope. But I can hope. And if it's not, the next one will be. Or the one after that."

She gasped. "How many kids do you plan on having?"

"I don't know yet. As many as you'll let me impregnate you with, I guess."

"Let's start with this one and then talk." She turned her head to one side and leaned her face against his chest as he hugged her tight.

"I love you, Ashley Harmon."

"I love you, too, Evan Harmon." Her breathing slowed. Finally she muttered into his chest. "We missed the sunset."

"We'll catch the next one. I hear it happens every day at about this time."

"Ha ha. You're so funny."

"We have a week. I want you to spend that time relaxing and worrying about nothing except gaining more strength, soaking up the sun, and staring at the sunsets. Leave the rest to me." He pulled her back to arm's length. "Deal?"

"Deal."

AUTHOR'S NOTE

I hope you've enjoyed this fourth book in the Wolf Gatherings series. Please enjoy the following excerpt from the fifth book in the series, *Abandoned*.

ABANDONED

WOLF GATHERINGS, BOOK FIVE

Allison huddled in the dark corner of the closet, shivering with cold. She kept her knees tucked under her chin, and her matted hair hung around her face. She couldn't remember when she'd last had a bath or washed her hair. She'd lost track of time. She didn't know how long she'd been in this dark prison, either. Hours? Days?

She was so thirsty. If she had to guess, it had been a few days. She'd slept only in short spurts, unable to get comfortable and repeatedly jerking awake out of fear. Even the slightest noise startled her.

She'd rocked to keep warm, but dressed only in shorts and a T-shirt, she wasn't wearing enough clothes for the lower temperatures she'd experienced...*wherever the hell I am.*

A noise made her freeze. She stiffened and lifted her face as though it would help her hear better. She held her breath. Was he back? He'd never left her this long. She didn't know which fate was worse, starving to death locked in this closet or him returning to drag her out and stab a needle into her filled with whatever he repeatedly injected into her.

He rarely spoke and never answered any of her questions. She'd given up trying to communicate or reason with him months ago. But she had no idea what his intentions were. She was stuck, seemingly in the middle of nowhere in a cabin in the woods. She thought they had traveled north that first night when someone snatched her from The Gathering last year, and the cooler weather would indicate she was right.

She'd been in her hotel room alone when a man knocked on the door, sweet-talked his way inside, and then jabbed her in the thigh with a syringe.

Her last memory had been staring at him wide-eyed as her body stopped holding itself upright. He'd cradled her in his arms and set her on the bed. Even her mouth refused to omit a scream. Everything had gone black.

She didn't know his name. Nor did she know the name of the man who had been her guard here in this cabin. He'd never told her. She knew it had been over a year, judging by the change of seasons.

The only clothes she had were the contents of the small suitcase she'd taken to The Gathering. Her captor had packed up all her belongings and taken her drugged body and everything she had with her. Unfortunately, The Gathering was held at the beginning of summer in Oklahoma. Nothing but warm-weather clothing accompanied her.

And now she was stuck without proper attire for the

weather, and the asshole holding her hostage never provided her with anything else.

When she'd awoken the day after her abduction, she found herself bound and gagged in the back of a Jeep bumping down the road toward her new fate. This was not what she'd had in mind when she'd gone to The Gathering.

Sure, she'd been looking for a mate. Every red-blooded shifter between the ages of eighteen and thirty did the same thing every other year when they attended. Anyone not interested in mating usually didn't show up.

But that man was not her mate. Nor was the man who'd kept her hostage in the cabin.

Footsteps… She angled her head toward the closet door. There were too many. More than one set. Every time there had been visitors, Allison had been on the receiving end of strange drugs that altered her state of mind and stole her memory.

Stomping and shuffling…even running… Someone was in a hurry. Whispers…

Allison grew anxious. She stiffened her spine. She reached out her tongue to lick her dry lips to no avail. Her saliva was almost nonexistent. A chill ran down her arms, and she squeezed her legs tighter.

"Is anybody here?" a voice bellowed.

Allison flinched. Fear made her keep very still. Nothing good happened when that closet door opened. She knew better than to trust whoever was on the other side of that door.

"Allison? Allison Watkins?" More shuffling around.

Something large scraped across the floor. The small kitchen table? "Shit."

Another deeper voice joined the first. Neither belonged to her captor. "Do you think we're too late? Fuck."

Could it be? Had someone finally found her?

Hope crawled up her spine and landed on her shoulders, weighing them down, pressing her into the floor. She couldn't lift her body, but she still had her voice. "In here." The words came out weak and raspy. She tried to lick her dry lips and opened her mouth again. "Here. I'm in here." This time she sounded louder.

"Allison?" Footsteps came closer. Thank God. At least she hoped she should be thanking God. The good intentions of these presumed rescuers had yet to be proven.

The closet door rattled. It was locked. Of course. For a moment she wondered if they thought she was stupid. If it hadn't been locked, she wouldn't still be sitting in the closet freezing her ass off. How did the closet always manage to stay colder than the rest of the cabin?

"Ma'am, could you get as far from the door as possible? I'm going to kick it in." The voice was soothing, but urgent. The fact that he'd addressed her as "ma'am" eased some of her suspicions. She hadn't been treated with any sort of humane respect in over a year.

Allison tucked her feet farther under her and pushed herself to standing. She was amazed she had the energy to pull herself upright, but adrenaline kicked in at the thought of being rescued. Finally.

She'd given up hope long ago.

Something hit the closet door and her body jerked. She squeezed herself tighter into the corner, but it was difficult to avoid the opening. The closet wasn't much larger than the door frame.

Two more times something slammed into the door before it splintered and broke free around the lock. Large hands reached inside and tugged the splintered wood until it gave way and daylight flooded her tiny cell.

Allison flung an arm over her face against the brightness. She'd been in the pitch dark too long.

"Are you Allison Watkins?" a voice asked.

"Ye-yes," she muttered, barely able to hear herself.

"You're safe now, ma'am. You can come out."

Allison peeked over her forearm, her eyes squinted against the light of day. In reality it wasn't that bright. She just wasn't accustomed to seeing at all.

Two men stood just outside the closet, both wearing hunting gear. No, not hunting clothes exactly, but camouflage. And they were armed. Military? They were shifters. Perhaps members of the North American Reserves, then? They stepped back and gave her space, the larger one holding his hand out toward her.

She stared at the gesture but didn't reach for him. Her heart pounded so hard she thought it might beat right out of her chest. She hadn't seen many people besides her captor in over a year. The only time others had visited, they hadn't spoken. They'd simply covered her head, taken her to some sort of medical lab, and then later returned her to the cabin. No one had ever addressed her or looked her in the eye.

This man was looking directly at her and concern furrowed his brow. He dropped his hand. "We're here to rescue you, Allison. You can trust us."

I've heard that before.

Allison stepped over the debris, trying to avoid the splintered wood with her bare feet.

There were three men in the room. One stood by the door, gun drawn, eyes scanning the outside. A knife hung at his waist and a larger rifle was strapped over his shoulder.

Allison shivered. She had no idea if she could trust these people, but she had nothing to lose, either.

The largest man spoke again. "I'm Bill. Are you all right?"

Allison glanced down at herself. "I think so." She licked her lips. "So thirsty."

The shorter blond man darted across to the sink in two strides, grabbed a glass from the counter, and filled it with water from the tap. "How long have you been in there?" he asked as he handed her the cold, welcome liquid.

Allison downed the entire thing in one long draw, knowing she shouldn't, but unable to stop herself. Her stomach would hurt, but she didn't care. "Not sure," she muttered. "Days?"

"Who brought you here?" the shorter blond asked. "I'm Chuck, by the way." He thumbed over his shoulder. "That's Marshall manning the door."

Marshall didn't turn around. She barely saw his profile. He had longer dark hair, almost black, and he was taller and slimmer.

"He never said his name." Allison narrowed her gaze at the three men one at a time, still trying to decide if these men had her best interest in mind.

"How long have you been here?" Chuck asked. He took the empty glass from her and lifted it. "Do you want more?"

She shook her head. She should wait a while before drinking more. "Since The Gathering. A year?" She wasn't positive. "Have...you been looking for me that long?"

"Not quite, but close." Chuck looked her up and down. "Is that all you have to wear?"

"Yes." Allison wrapped her arms around her middle and shivered again at the mention. "He never gave me more than I had at The Gathering."

The bigger man, Bill, shrugged quickly out of his jacket and draped it around her shoulders. "It's not much, but it'll help."

Marshall nodded outside as he cleared his throat. "Let's get out of here." He glanced at Allison and then back out the opening to the outside. "When do you expect your captor to return?"

"No idea. He's been gone longer than usual. I was beginning to think he'd left me for dead." She stared at Marshall's back, attempting to keep her breathing steady. She was scared out of her mind. *They offered you water and gave you a coat. Surely they don't intend to kill you.*

"Is there anything you want to take?" Chuck asked.

Allison glanced around. "No." She wouldn't mind having at least her purse with her identification, but she had no idea where it was or even if it still existed. "Who are you guys? You don't look like police." Was she trading one problem for another? She'd been held captive for a year by one man. There were three here now. They weren't official by any means. Just three men who thought they'd swoop in and take her to another location. *Shifters, though.* That had to mean something.

But three men had come in several times and taken her to another location and then returned her. She could hardly remember the details of any of those encounters.

"We aren't with the human police. We're hired by The Head Council." Chuck stepped closer to the door and then turned from her to Marshall. "Ready?"

"Clear." Marshall pushed the door all the way open and eased outside.

"I'll explain better in the car," Chuck continued over his shoulder. "I know you're scared and I don't blame you, but I swear we're the good guys. And we don't want to be anywhere near here when your kidnapper returns."

Allison didn't think he would return at all, but that wasn't going to stop her from getting the hell out of there. She couldn't imagine a fate worse than staying right then. "He wasn't my kidnapper. Another man took me from The Gathering and brought me here. I don't know who either of them were."

"I'm so sorry, ma'am." Bill ducked his head. "Our mission is rescue. Someone else will come behind us to investigate the scene."

Allison looked down at her feet. "How far do we

have to walk? I'm not very strong." She hadn't eaten anything in days and not enough for a regular person in a year. She spotted her tennis shoes by the front door and slipped them on. At least her feet would be protected.

"We have an SUV very close. We didn't want to pull up to the door, but close enough to walk." Bill set a hand on her shoulder and she flinched.

"Let's go." Marshall took off. He scanned every direction and kept low, his knees bent as he jogged away from the cabin.

Chuck followed on his heels. "Stay right behind me."

Allison stepped outside. Her legs wobbled after so long crouched in the closet and not enough use for months. She hadn't even been outside in a long time. When her captor was home, she was permitted to use the tiny bathroom in one corner of the cabin, the only separate room it contained. When he was away and she was locked in the closet, she peed in a bucket in the cramped space. She always knew when she was dehydrated because she no longer needed to pee.

She soon saw the black SUV they'd mentioned among the trees about twenty yards away. Her legs threatened to buckle, but adrenaline pulled her along.

She couldn't imagine anyone was watching them or following them, but she felt the palpable concern of the three men flanking her.

Allison scanned in both directions. The hairs on the back of her neck prickled, and she tripped over a tree stump. Chuck reached back and swept her off her feet before she hit the ground.

And then all hell broke loose. A shot rang out. And then another, coming from the opposite direction. It happened so fast, Allison couldn't tell for sure where the noises came from.

Chuck flattened her against the ground, lying on top of her and covering her head. Her knees hit the dirt hard, and then her face. She took a deep breath and dust filled her nose.

More shots. So many she couldn't count them. She could see Marshall's boots to her side where he crouched down in front of her face and mowed the area with his machine gun.

Her chest pounded. She couldn't breathe. Chuck was pressing on top of her with too much weight. And she blinked, but dirt clouded her vision, making her eyes burn.

A loud grunt followed by a thump filtered into her awareness. Bill. Had he been hit?

Allison pushed against the ground with both hands, trying to free herself of Chuck's overpowering pressure on her back. She couldn't get him to budge.

"Go," Marshall whispered. He glanced back at Chuck and then down at Allison. She squinted to see him. "Get her to the SUV. I'll be right behind you." He motioned with his chin toward the tree line.

Chuck whisked her off the ground as though she weighed nothing. He held her against his chest, one arm wrapped around her middle. Her feet didn't reach the ground.

"Go with them," Marshall said. He must have spoken that last part to Bill. "Hurry."

When they reached the car, Bill stepped around Chuck and whipped open the back door. Chuck swung her inside. "Get on the floor," he muttered before he slammed the door. Within seconds all three men had circled to the other doors and jumped inside. Someone started the SUV and gunned the engine so fast, Allison had to brace herself against the front seat. She squeezed into a tight ball on the floor and ducked her head, expecting the glass to shatter all around her any moment.

The ride was rough at first as the SUV bounced around on the uneven ground. There were no more shots. She held her breath for several minutes it seemed, worried about a tire blowing or the gas tank exploding. Whatever sorts of things might happen to a car in a gun fight.

When she finally tipped her head up, she saw Bill in the seat across from her. His gaze kept shifting from one window to another, scanning the area behind them as they sped away. He held his left arm tight with his right hand wrapped around his bicep. Blood trickled between his fingers. He didn't seem to notice.

With a huge bounce, the SUV went over a large bump and then the drive smoothed out. They must have hit the pavement.

"I think we're safe now," Marshall said over his shoulder. "You okay, Bill?"

"Yeah, just a flesh wound. I'll live." He unwrapped his fingers from his arm and peeked at the damage, making Allison's stomach revolt. She'd never seen a gunshot wound before. And she couldn't see anything but blood on his jacket now. But the idea of what lay beneath made her swallow back bile.

"Who was that?" Allison asked, dipping her gaze down so she could avoid staring at Bill's wound.

"No idea," Chuck said from the front. "But they didn't like the idea of us taking you, that's for sure."

She breathed a giant sigh of relief. Whatever the fuck that chapter in her life had been, she hoped it was over. She lifted her gaze back to Bill. "Where are you taking me?"

ALSO BY BECCA JAMESON

Canyon Springs:

Caleb's Mate

Hunter's Mate

Corked and Tapped:

Volume One: Friday Night

Volume Two: Company Party

Volume Three: The Holidays

Surrender:

Raising Lucy

Teaching Abby

Leaving Roman

Project DEEP:

Reviving Emily

Reviving Trish

Reviving Dade

Reviving Zeke

Reviving Graham

Reviving Bianca

Reviving Olivia

Project DEEP Box Set One

Project DEEP Box Set Two

SEALs in Paradise:

Hot SEAL, Red Wine

Hot SEAL, Australian Nights

Hot SEAL, Cold Feet

Dark Falls:

Dark Nightmares

Club Zodiac:

Training Sasha

Obeying Rowen

Collaring Brooke

Mastering Rayne

Trusting Aaron

Claiming London

Sharing Charlotte

Taming Rex

Tempting Elizabeth

Club Zodiac Box Set One

Club Zodiac Box Set Two

The Art of Kink:

Pose

Paint

Sculpt

Arcadian Bears:

Grizzly Mountain

Grizzly Beginning

Grizzly Secret

Grizzly Promise

Grizzly Survival

Grizzly Perfection

Arcadian Bears Box Set One

Arcadian Bears Box Set Two

Sleeper SEALs:

Saving Zola

Spring Training:

Catching Zia

Catching Lily

Catching Ava

Spring Training Box Set

The Underground series:

Force

Clinch

Guard

Submit

Thrust

Torque

The Underground Box Set One

The Underground Box Set Two

Saving Sofia (Special Forces: Operations Alpha)

Wolf Masters series:

Kara's Wolves

Lindsey's Wolves

Jessica's Wolves

Alyssa's Wolves

Tessa's Wolf

Rebecca's Wolves

Melinda's Wolves

Laurie's Wolves

Amanda's Wolves

Sharon's Wolves

Wolf Masters Box Set One

Wolf Masters Box Set Two

Claiming Her series:

The Rules

The Game

The Prize

Emergence series:

Bound to be Taken

Bound to be Tamed

Bound to be Tested

Bound to be Tempted

Emergence Box Set

The Fight Club series:

Come

Perv

Need

Hers

Want

Lust

The Fight Club Box Set One

The Fight Club Box Set Two

Wolf Gatherings series:

Tarnished

Dominated

Completed

Redeemed

Abandoned

Betrayed

Wolf Gatherings Box Set One

Wolf Gathering Box Set Two

Durham Wolves series:

Rescue in the Smokies

Fire in the Smokies

Freedom in the Smokies

Stand Alone Books:

Blind with Love

Guarding the Truth

Out of the Smoke

Abducting His Mate

Three's a Cruise

Wolf Trinity

Frostbitten

A Princess for Cale/A Princess for Cain

ABOUT THE AUTHOR

Becca Jameson is a USA Today best-selling author of over 100 books. She is well-known for her Wolf Masters series, her Fight Club series, and her Club Zodiac series. She currently lives in Houston, Texas, with her husband and her Goldendoodle. Two grown kids pop in every once in a while too! She is loving this journey and has dabbled in a variety of genres, including paranormal, sports romance, military, and BDSM.

A total night owl, Becca writes late at night, sequestering herself in her office with a glass of red wine and a bar of dark chocolate, her fingers flying across the keyboard as her characters weave their own stories.

During the day--which never starts before ten in the morning!--she can be found jogging, running errands, or reading in her favorite hammock chair!

...*where Alphas dominate*...

Becca's Newsletter Sign-up:
http://beccajameson.com/newsletter-sign-up

Join my Facebook fan group, Becca's Bibliomaniacs,

for the most up-to-date information, random excerpts while I work, giveaways, and fun release parties!

Facebook Fan Group:
https://www.facebook.com/groups/BeccasBibliomaniacs/

Contact Becca:
www.beccajameson.com
beccajameson4@aol.com

- facebook.com/becca.jameson.18
- twitter.com/beccajameson
- instagram.com/becca.jameson
- bookbub.com/authors/becca-jameson
- goodreads.com/beccajameson
- amazon.com/author/beccajameson